By the same author

The Killer's Cousin
Locked Inside

BLACK MIRROR

NANCY WERLIN

Collins flamingo

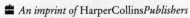
An imprint of HarperCollins*Publishers*

First published in the USA by Dial Books 2001
Dial Books is a division of Penguin Putnam Inc.
First published in Great Britain by CollinsFlamingo 2003
CollinsFlamingo is an imprint of HarperCollins*Publishers* Ltd,
77-85 Fulham Palace Road, Hammersmith, London W6 8JB

The HarperCollins website address is
www.harpercollins.co.uk

1 3 5 7 9 8 6 4 2

Text copyright © Nancy Werlin 2001

The author asserts the moral right to be
identified as the author of the work.

ISBN 0 00 714168 8

Printed and bound in England by
Clays Ltd, St Ives plc

For my editor, Lauri Hornik, with appreciation,
and continued astonishment at my good luck

Have you ever been in a state of pain so intense, it was like a living creature wound tightly around your ribcage and shoulders and neck? Getting into that place requires not just one thing that's wrong, but instead a whole tangled *knot* of wrongness. It requires wrong things you've done, along with wrong things that have been done to you. It requires both good and bad intentions, doubled and tripled back upon themselves until they're so distorted, you can't see clearly where they began. It requires wrong decisions, but no vision of what other choices you might have made. It requires you to see every inadequacy, every failing, every weakness you possess, magnified to horrific size. It requires bad luck. And then, when you reach this place and look round, you see only blackness. And only one possible route to travel: downward, and inward, into more blackness.

1

Seven years ago, when I was only nine and we had just moved into her house, Bubbe stood me in front of her. Seated in her chair, she could still look straight into my face, and then her eyes narrowed as she looked me up and down. "Frances," she announced sternly, "you may have her delicate face and bones, but you are *not* going to be a dainty Japanese woman like your mother. You're going to be a typical voluptuous Leventhal." She put her hands measuringly on my hips and added disapprovingly: "And soon."

Bubbe, my father's mother, was of course a Leventhal only by marriage. Her statement felt to me like the curse of an evil fairy. Within weeks I menstruated for the first time, and also discovered that I was one of those women plagued by vicious monthly cramps. And naturally, it didn't end there. My waist nipped in, my hips rounded, and my breasts swelled suddenly and painfully, so that for a while I had to clutch them to my chest with one arm when going up and down stairs.

Even before this I'd known myself to be somewhat strange in appearance. Yes, there was a strong facial resemblance to my mother. But other things about me made people blink, or frown in puzzlement. I'd seen the discreet double takes. I'd been asked countless times: "Where are you *from*?" I certainly didn't appear Caucasian – that is, typically "American" – and I didn't fit a single stereotype of what a Jew ought to look like. All would have been well if I had just looked Japanese, but there was also something about my looks that didn't fit what people expected from a child of Asian ancestry. Something that seemed a little... off.

My premature maturity made things worse. It wasn't just the uncomfortable weirdness of my changing body, or Bubbe's patent disapproval, or even the fact that my father abruptly stopped being able to hug me. There was also an incident that I could not forget.

It happened a few months after we'd moved to Lattimore. I was waiting in a grocery line, holding our place while my father ran back for orange juice, when I noticed two women in the next line pointing. And then whispering.

"What *is* she? Some kind of Asian?"

"Yes, I guess – although, that hair? A mix? I don't know. But, oh, look at the breasts. I could cry."

"I *know*! She's so tiny, they make her look like a dwarf."

"Poor freaky kid."

"Yeah."

As soon as I got back to Bubbe's, I locked myself in the upstairs bathroom. I had planned to take off all my clothes, stand on the step stool, and look at myself, naked, in the mirror above the sink. But I didn't. Instead I sat on the closed lid of the toilet and cried. In my mind I could hear those two women. And after that I began wearing big, baggy clothes and avoiding mirrors.

It was also around this time that my brother, Daniel, and I began to suspect that our move from Cambridge to rural, dying Lattimore was permanent, and that our father honestly didn't have a clue if our enigmatic mother would ever decide to come back from her Buddhist monastery in Osaka.

More importantly, that was when I began to draw.

I drew anything. Everything. Doodles at first. But I had a knack for reproducing what I saw, and soon my paper and pencil – and then later, my paints and charcoals – formed a strong, protective wall around me. They stood between me and everyone else in the world. I liked it that way. I liked being quiet, letting no one know what I thought, or how ferocious those thoughts were.

I let no one know, that is, but my brother. Just ten months older than me, and in the same grade at school (and, through some genetic freakishness, tall and mostly Caucasian-looking), Daniel was my best and only friend. Daniel was the only person with whom I was willing to share my real self, the Frances who was behind my wall of art, my habitual quiet mask. The real me. Me, Frances. Frances, who was screaming and angry inside. Frances, who was just... waiting, although I wasn't sure what I was waiting for.

Yes, when we were first living with Bubbe, I had been able to talk to Daniel. He had meant so much to me. And yet, after we began at The Pettengill School, two years ago, I hadn't been able to stop our closeness from slipping away, until it was irretrievably gone.

I used to blame Pettengill for that. I used to blame Saskia. Saskia, and Daniel's friends in the Unity Service charitable group at school. I'd blamed Patrick Leyden, the entrepreneur who'd founded Unity and who Daniel longed to emulate. And, of course, I'd blamed Daniel himself.

I used to blame anyone but myself.

But now that Daniel is gone, I know better. My brother is dead of a massive, self-injected dose of heroin, and the only note he left behind was for Saskia. My brother was in pain, and I noticed nothing. *Nothing.*

2

Everyone who was anyone at The Pettengill School showed up at Bubbe's house on the last night we sat shivah for Daniel. Some had come earlier in the week as well, but they seemed to think it was important to return on this final night. I helped with food and drinks. I was, in fact, nearly crazed after the empty days in which neither my father nor Bubbe had anything to say. Crazed with my own ceaseless circling anguish. It was a relief to have people around. "Cookie?" I asked person after person, quietly. "Chocolate chip? Mint Milano? Peanut butter? Please have another."

In the hall I let my eyes rest on the black-draped mirror. I had a fleeting wish that it, and all mirrors, could stay that way always. I didn't want, even by accident, to catch a glimpse of myself.

I kept looking for Daniel's girlfriend, Saskia. I was girding myself to approach her tonight, even though I knew she would be surrounded by her friends. Unity, the charitable group. Daniel's friends too, of course. I had never liked Saskia, and I knew that she despised me. But now... now.

I took a deep breath. I continued to circulate as I waited for her to arrive. I nodded, allowed myself to be gently hugged, to have my hands pressed and my face examined minutely. It felt odd, everyone being so nice. I didn't know if I liked it. I had become accustomed to being ignored at school.

When would Saskia arrive?

I listened while Brenda Delahay told me at length how much she would miss Daniel. How kind he had been, how caring, how unusual that was. She washed down seven mint Milano cookies with Diet Coke. Then she excused herself. I watched her stick legs mount the stairs towards the bathroom and wondered if what I'd overheard about her was true. It had been Daniel who'd said it, under his breath to Saskia as our class waited for history to start. After Brenda had come running in, looking very pale, and slipped into her seat.

When's she going to figure out that it's easier to do speed than throw up? Maybe somebody should ease her in with some diet pills.

Not so kind, not so caring – in fact, a rotten, mean joke for Daniel to make. But I knew no boy could possibly understand the importance of being slender. Not the way girls understood. And Daniel had liked thin girls – you had only to look at Saskia.

I realised I'd put my hand tentatively on my own round hip. I snatched it away. I swivelled. "Cookie?" I said randomly to the group of kids behind me.

"Sure," said James Droussian. I noticed he was drinking milk, of all things. He took two cookies, said, "Thanks, Frances," and grinned appreciatively right at me. And I felt my cheeks warm uncontrollably in response.

James just... well. There was that adorable brown ponytail,

and the cheekbones so defined that they looked like they could cut paper. He talked easily to anyone, as if he didn't have a clue that there were groups and cliques. On top of that, there was the way he smiled. For an instant his eyes looked directly into yours and said silently: *You.*

And you couldn't help feeling, for that instant, that he truly thought you were interesting. That he couldn't *wait* to get to know you.

Of course I knew better. James Droussian had only come to Pettengill this past fall, but it was already an open secret that he dealt drugs. He never touched anything himself, never urged anything on anyone. But he always had a little something around. So it was his *business* to have people like him, to charm people, and it didn't matter who they were, so long as they could pay. He was everybody's friend, James, and that smile of his – it was meaningless.

I turned my back on James and his little circle of burnouts. Then, for the first time, it occurred to me to wonder exactly where Daniel had got the smack he'd overdosed on. Was it possible James had sold – no. I dismissed the thought immediately. Daniel had had no more money that I had, and I'd heard that James didn't do samples. I'd always thought Daniel had got his marijuana from friends, free. Someone must have given him the heroin as well. Who? And did I even *want* to know? What difference did it make, after all? It wouldn't bring him back to life, or change the facts about me. My brother had had a major habit, and I'd thought he only smoked some occasional marijuana.

Suddenly I heard Daniel's voice in my mind, jeering the way he used to: *Frances, cultivate mindfulness.* I felt my shoulders hunch defensively. After our mother left, Daniel had memorised literally hundreds of Buddhist aphorisms and catchphrases, from the profound to the preposterous. He had quoted them mockingly at every opportunity, driving me – and our father – nearly crazy.

I practically ran into the foyer with my now-empty plate of cookies.

I was just in time to put the plate down and greet a little circle of Pettengill teachers and administrators, who were trickling in from the front porch where they'd been stamping the snow off their boots. Headmaster Ferkell and his wife, who taught chemistry. Ancient Mrs Kingston, Latin. Mr Dickenson and Ms Polke, history. Mr Prodanas, maths.

And then Patrick Leyden came in, looking thin and dapper and self-assured in one of his expensive wool suits. But, as always, I had to work not to stare at his earlobes. They were round and fleshy and swung slightly whenever he moved his head. Even tonight my fingers itched to draw a vicious caricature.

Daniel's voice sneered again in my head. *A disciplined mind leads to happiness.*

More Pettengill teachers streamed in steadily, looking down into my face and pressing my hands (the men) or stooping to hug me (the women). All of them saying nice things about Daniel. I searched surreptitiously for my art teacher, Ms Wiles. Finally I spotted her, looking especially young and pretty with snowflakes melting on her cinnamon hair. She was standing beside Patrick Leyden, who was talking at her nonstop. As if she felt my gaze, Ms Wiles looked up and nodded, solemnly, directly at me. I nodded back, and the moment was like a sudden oasis in the noise and confusion and pain.

Sometimes I felt sure that Ms Wiles could just look at me and understand things I hadn't even fully formulated. Not that she ever said them aloud. She just... looked. As now. I can't explain it. Yvette Wiles was just... special. We could be silent together.

Sometimes I wished I could *be* her.

As the stream of adults ended, I spotted Saskia across the room. She was with a few of her friends. Unity Service folks, as I'd expected. Wallace Chan. George de Witt, who was the Vice President of Unity. A couple others.

I wanted to talk to Saskia; I had planned to talk to her, but my stomach roiled anyway. Shame swept over me. How could I say what I wanted to say? How would she react? Maybe I shouldn't – maybe I couldn't...

Unity Service. Why, freshman year, had I so stubbornly refused to help out with their food and clothing drives for the poor, their scholarship fundraisers? Unity Service was a big deal. Although only a few years old, it had become the largest and most respected student-run charitable group in the country. They'd funded my own scholarship, among so many others, but still I kept saying no. No, no, no. Even Daniel hadn't been able to sway me. I'd just kept repeating that I wasn't a joiner.

If I said now that I'd changed my mind, would they scorn me?

We wouldn't have you now if you begged to join, Daniel had told me last year. *You're the only scholarship recipient in Unity's history who hasn't joined the organisation. Who hasn't helped out, who hasn't given back. I'm actually ashamed of my own sister! Art doesn't help anyone, you know. It doesn't give people jobs, or food, or clothes, or opportunities. Business joined to charity does that.*

Business joined to charity. Those words were a straight quote from Patrick Leyden, and when Daniel quoted Leyden, he didn't mock.

I wanted to talk to Saskia. Ethereal dark-haired Saskia Sweeney, unrecognisable as the poor girl from Lattimore she'd once been. Saskia, Daniel's girlfriend, of whom I'd been so jealous. Who, I'd thought, had stolen my brother's companionship and love from me. I wanted to beg for forgiveness. I wanted to be her friend. But I – I couldn't. Not tonight.

I turned abruptly and slipped past them all, outside Bubbe's house, into the cold winter air.

3

Bubbe's house is an old Victorian with a wraparound porch. I ran quickly to the side of the house, where I was less likely to be seen and spoken to. I stood still. The cold air felt wonderful; I gripped my coatless arms and breathed it in. I stared out at the blanket of snow glittering on the ground beneath the moon and wondered: when I got up the nerve to talk to Saskia, how would she react? Did she hate me?

I felt a gentle touch on my shoulder and whipped round, my whole body stiffening with anxiety. I wasn't ready!

But it wasn't Saskia who had touched me so tentatively. It was only Andy Jankowski. He had taken off his coat and was holding it out to me. Behind me I saw the porch swing still moving gently and realised that he must have been sitting out here, alone.

I gathered myself. "Hi there, Andy," I said awkwardly. "I'm not cold."

Andy nodded as if he understood me, but he still held the coat out. He's a big, heavy, strong man in his forties, with a deep wrinkle of worry engraved permanently across his forehead. He was wearing layers of flannel shirts; I could count at least three, all identical red and black plaid. He continued to extend the coat towards me, and after a few seconds I felt churlish for continuing to refuse. I slipped the coat on. It was a wool pea coat that fell nearly to my ankles, the sleeves went inches and inches past my hands. It smelled of recent dry cleaning.

I looked at Andy. "Thanks," I said uncertainly, and he nodded and turned a little aside, looking out again over the snow.

I thought about urging Andy inside the house so that I could be alone. But somehow I couldn't get the words out, so we just stood, side by side, and stared in the direction of Pettengill. In the moonlight ahead, I could clearly see the white steeple of the school chapel.

Andy is a "gifted arborist", the Headmaster was known for saying, "whom Pettengill is very lucky indeed to employ". The Headmaster always made a real point of this, especially with new students, though I believe it had been a long time since any students tormented Andy. In the past I had only said "Hello" and "How are you?" to him and to the other "special" employee at the school, a woman who worked in the kitchen. But right now, standing next to Andy and looking out over the snowy night, I was filled with a kind of peace. This was one person who wasn't going to say meaninglessly: "Please let me know if there's anything I can do." I could stand there and think my own thoughts. About... No, I would not think about Saskia. Not right now. But about my brother and how The Pettengill School had changed our lives, as freshmen, two years ago.

Pettengill is so close, physically, to the dying town of Lattimore. And yet, it's located on a different planet.

Pettengill is a private preparatory school. It is quite beautiful. It boasts one of the most acclaimed Georgian campuses in New England. There are no fewer than five brick quadrangles, and in the summer and fall most of the buildings are covered with luxuriant old-growth ivy. The grounds – thanks at least in part to Andy Jankowski – are immaculate, the privileged students and faculty are well-dressed and energetic, full of life, vibrant.

But from the other edge of the campus, in winter, when there's no screen of foliage, you have a clear view of the boarded-up windows of Lattimore's old shoe factories. Nothing could look more dead than those buildings. Nothing could be more of a contrast.

When we were much younger and had just come to live in the town of Lattimore, Daniel used to stare whenever we drove by Leventhal Shoes. The name had been painted large in white on the brick side of one of the midsize factories, but by the time we moved to town, the paint had faded and a few of the letters were completely missing. Bubbe had stayed on in Lattimore after Zayde died and the factory closed, rattling around in her big house, too stubborn and too old, she said, to go elsewhere.

When we moved in with her after our mother left, our father claimed that Bubbe needed us. "I can write my novels anywhere," he said, "and my mother needs the company and the care."

This last was an outright lie, though I've never been sure if my father allowed himself to know it. Bubbe – and I resented the fact that she'd appropriated a title that ought to be grandmotherly, affectionate – was in perfect health. Moreover, she was the most unsociable, unneedy person I've ever met, with the possible exception of my mother. But unlike my mother, Bubbe was cutting rather than detached. She called it honest, of course. Forthright.

It was Bubbe's opinion that my mother's call to spirituality was a cover for the fact that she had got tired of supporting my father's delusions as he wrote one after another obscure, unreadable, low-paying, and eventually unpublishable science fiction novel. Daniel and I knew this was Bubbe's opinion because she aired it regularly. It was one of the reasons – one of the many, many reasons – that we were overjoyed when Pettengill – well, actually Unity Service – made their offer to the dying town of Lattimore.

"Through the generous offices of our chapter of the Unity Service Foundation, headed by Pettengill board member and Internet entrepreneur Patrick Leyden, our school has the resources," declared the announcement in the *Lattimore Weekly News*, "and our local students have the need. We will join forces for the future so that all our children, rich and poor, have access to the best possible education."

It was a forward-thinking, heart-warming and generous concept on the part of Unity Service, said the local – and then suddenly the national – news media. It was a shining example of the power of young people to do good. Donations poured into the Unity Service coffers, and within months Unity chapters around the country were setting similar programmes in place. New Unity chapters sprouted up overnight. There'd been articles in many major newspapers, magazines and websites. And at the end of last year the President of the United States had actually given the organisation, in the person of Patrick Leyden, a Freedom Award.

At the time, however, all Daniel and I thought about was that we were miraculously enabled to move out of Bubbe's house. "Unity scholarship students at Pettengill will belong to the regular boarding student body, with full access to the school's myriad programmes and facilities." It was the escape from Bubbe's house that Daniel and I had dreamed of, and it had come years earlier than we had believed possible.

Of course, we'd had no idea how it would actually *feel* for us to be on Unity scholarships. No idea at all. Freshman year, we were completely at the bottom of the Pettengill social barrel. And we were supposed to be grateful for it too. Daniel had been. Saskia, who was also from the town of Lattimore, had been. But I—

I shivered. What was wrong with me?

"...cold?"

It took me a moment to realise that Andy had spoken. Before I knew it, he was offering to give me one of his shirts too. "No, no," I said quickly. "I'm not cold. Your coat is wonderfully warm. I was just thinking about something."

"Oh," said Andy. He returned to being silent. I was abruptly aware that Andy would have given me all his shirts and never suggested that I go inside. I was filled with a new appreciation for him. Whatever his disabilities – some kind of mild mental retardation, I supposed – Andy Jankowski was a person who wouldn't hurt, wouldn't betray.

"Thank you for coming over tonight, Andy," I said.

He began absently to strike his left forearm with the open palm of his right hand. "My father died," he said. "And now Debbie is gone. She might be dead too. I don't know."

I looked the long distance up at him. His profile was impassive. I didn't know what to say. Even if I had known, I was suddenly incapable of speech.

"When you're dead," Andy added, "people can't see you ever again. And they miss you."

I turned my head away. The moonlit glare off the snow hurt my eyes. I hugged Andy's coat round myself and stood quite still next to him on the porch.

Sweet and clear came a voice behind us. "Frances?" said Saskia Sweeney. "Please, can we speak?"

4

Eleanor Roosevelt once said: "No one can make you feel inferior without your consent." I've read several biographies about her. She was plain and intense. When she and her beautiful, popular cousin Alice were society debutantes, Alice laughed at Eleanor and told everyone she was boring. Eleanor felt inferior then, I'm certain. She tried to hide.

I wonder – looking at pictures of the mature Eleanor, with her buck teeth and her hunched posture and her stubborn, thoughtful eyes – if her feelings of inferiority ever truly changed, at base? Completely? I just don't see how they could have.

I know that's not the popular view. I know that's not what we wish to believe.

I was overwhelmingly conscious, as I slowly turned to face Saskia Sweeney, that she, and not I, would be the one of whom Eleanor Roosevelt would approve. Beautiful Saskia (with the Pre-Raphaelite heaps of hair, and the wide-set eyes, and the creamy skin, and the tall slender body, and, somehow, the exactly-right clothes) was also Saskia of the warm heart and the open hands. Who on earth wouldn't approve of the tirelessly do-gooding

Student President of the Pettengill chapter of Unity Service?

Me. That was who. And even though I'd vowed to change, it was Saskia who had come to look for *me* tonight, not the other way around. In my head Daniel's voice jeered: *Oh, Frances! A* bhikkhu *who envies others does not achieve stillness of mind.*

"I'm sorry for barging in on you," Saskia said, "but, well, I needed to tell you that—" Suddenly she looked disconcerted. "Andy! I was so focused on Frances, I didn't notice you at first." I saw her eyes flick over Andy's coat as it hung about me and then her smile flashed brighter than ever. "I see you're taking good care of Frances! Isn't she lucky to have a friend like you!"

For some reason I always heard subtle slurs, condescension, a malicious little something, twisted into whatever Saskia said. Daniel had jumped down my throat the one time I mentioned it. It was a month into our first term at Pettengill. He had said I was jealous of her. *She* was never anything but kind to everyone else, he said, no matter how freakish they might be. In fact, she was extra kind in that case.

You know that, Frances. I mean, she even sat down next to you at lunch the other day! Or last week, whenever it was. What more do you want? Why are you always so negative about everyone? If there's anyone you ought to feel comfortable with, it's Saskia. You're not even trying here!

I wanted to change. I did.

I said, "I'm glad you came out here, Saskia. I wanted to say something to you tonight, but I felt awkward..."

"I understand." Saskia stepped forward. She is one of those people who always stands a half-step too close. She looked down earnestly into my face. "Don't feel awkward. Please. I – we're both grieving. I know that. Whatever our differences, Frances – we both loved Daniel."

Her gaze was very intense. I felt like an ant captured beneath a magnifying glass. I was even more ashamed of myself than before. *I should have been the one saying these things to* her.

"Thank you," I managed. "I know you cared for him. And I know—" Involuntarily, I found I had taken a step back. "I know he cared a great deal about you."

I thought I heard the porch swing creak, and I guessed that Andy had sat back down there. Vaguely I wished he had not left my side.

Saskia said nothing, but all at once she enveloped me in a quick, light embrace. I wasn't prepared. I stiffened. I did not embrace her back. She felt my rejection, and stepped away herself. Her face was as rigid as mine now. "Well, that's all I had to say." She turned.

"Wait!" I said.

I thought she wouldn't, but then she did turn back. I searched desperately for words. "Thanks for coming out here. For talking to me."

"It's nothing."

Not her fault that I heard *You're nothing.*

I swallowed. "Saskia. I heard that Unity Service was planning to do some kind of... of memorial for Daniel. Is that true?"

"Yes," Saskia said after a moment. Her voice was very reserved now. "People seem to think it would be a nice gesture.

We're not sure yet what it will be. Some kind of project, probably."

"Well, I was wondering... um, that is – could I help? I'd like to be part of that."

Saskia's mouth literally dropped open in astonishment.

I hurried on. "I know it will look odd. I know I haven't had anything to do with Unity before. But – well, this is for Daniel, and besides that, I really would like to help out. I'd do anything."

There. However clumsily, I had said it. But as the silence continued, I felt a slow flush begin to cover my face.

"I'm sorry, Frances. I – people are very sorry for you, but I don't think that... well, I have to be honest here. You haven't been a part of Unity, and Daniel was, and people might resent – I mean... oh, God. This is difficult."

I blurted, "I was only thinking that—"

Saskia cut me off. "I'm sorry, Frances. I'll ask people, but I just don't think you'd be welcome." She had taken a step or two forward again. She put her hand on my arm. "I'm sorry. I really am. Maybe you and I can figure out something else, some other way that—"

I found myself ducking down and darting sideways, away from Saskia. She looked startled. I backed away even more, skidding a little on the light drifts of snow that had settled on the porch floorboards. "OK, I have to go inside now," I said. "I just came out to get some air, but my father will be wondering where I am – there's people to talk to. It's OK, about Unity. About the memorial. It was just an idea."

"But, Frances..."

From the corner of my eye I saw Andy, sitting on the swing with his feet positioned carefully below him, for all the world as if he were ready to jump up at a moment's notice. Jump to my defence. Now there was a preposterous thought. I somehow managed to smile at him. Then I looked back at Saskia. "I've got to go now," I said, and backed away. Away, away.

Inside, the house was even more densely packed with people than it had been before. I was conscious that Andy had silently followed me in and, obscurely, I was glad. I'd get him some cookies. I kept my head down. I made my way through the crowds as quickly as I could, trying to think only of getting cookies to give Andy.

But when I saw that the downstairs bathroom was unoccupied, instead I slipped inside and closed the door and locked it. I leaned against it. I held my elbows and took in some deep breaths. I closed my eyes. I breathed.

Occasions of hatred are certainly never settled by hatred. They are settled by freedom from hatred. This is the eternal law.

Shut up, Daniel, I thought. Shut up!

Tomorrow I would go back to school.

5

Long is the night for the sleepless.

At three in the morning nearly a week later, I gave up and turned on my bedside lamp. I looked round my little shoebox-shaped dorm room and thought about how much it had pleased me, once upon a time. Freshman year I'd worked hard to imprint my own personality on the room — the first room that had ever felt wholly mine, even if it did really belong to Pettengill. I'd liked the result so much that I'd declined to enter the upperclassman lottery for a bigger room. Even now, sleepless, thinking obsessively about Daniel, I was insensibly comforted by being there, under the threadbare but beautiful blue and white pinwheel quilt I'd found at a yard sale, with the plain white cotton pillows around me. I kept the room impeccably clean and neat. Coming here during the day between classes and meals and enforced activities, being here at night... kept me sane. Even during the moment of silence in Daniel's memory at this week's school assembly, I had been able to imagine myself here, alone. Safe.

Sitting up in bed, I tightened my arms round my stomach. I

had cramps, but they actually weren't too bad this time, and I knew they weren't the cause of my wakefulness. In the dimness, I could see the shadowy edges of the two blue rag rugs that warmed the floor, of the school-provided computer on my desk, of the big acrylic paintings on the walls.

Until now the acrylics, which I had joyously laboured over in the art studio, were the only things I'd allowed on the walls. I'd loved the contrast of the ferocious acrylics with the gentle quilt and rugs. And I'd loved Ms Wiles for her reaction to them. I'd shown them to her, shyly, when she came to Pettengill to teach. She hadn't made the mistake of thinking my paintings were simply blank dark squares. "Good God, Frances," she'd said. "You can *live* with those? They don't give you nightmares?"

I'd shaken my head, and she'd laughed a little. Except for Daniel, early freshman year, she was the only person I'd ever invited into my room.

But now something else had joined the acrylic paintings on the walls. I didn't really want to look at the new addition, but I did. It was an oval mirror, swiped from my room at Bubbe's. I had put it up here, and draped it in the black of mourning. A length of black silk, also swiped from Bubbe's. I supposed I could have chosen Buddhist white, rather than Jewish black, but the black had been available. And it didn't really matter to me which religion I expressed mourning in. The cloth was a *personal* symbol. It was so that I would have a visible reminder of Daniel's death at all times. It was so that I would remember my failure.

In the past days back at school I had made no progress in becoming more like the sister that Daniel would have wanted, the sister who might have helped him, the sister in whom he might have confided. I had tried, feebly. Instead of sitting alone at meals, I had steeled myself to go over and sit with some other kids. I'd tried various groups. The studious geeks one day. The burnouts another. The music freaks on a third occasion. Even the artsy types, a group with which anyone would have thought I'd fit in smoothly. But I didn't. I didn't fit in anywhere.

No one told me to go away or indicated in any way that I wasn't welcome. In fact, everybody was scrupulously polite to me. But all I could do was listen to the other kids talk about things I didn't care about or was not part of. Who was seeing whom. SATs. Weekend plans. I couldn't make myself participate. And I could tell they wondered what I was doing there.

The one group I took care to avoid, however, was probably the one I should most have persisted with. But after Saskia's rebuff, I didn't have the nerve to approach Daniel's friends from the Unity Service charity group. I did imagine, once or twice, that they were looking over at me. One evening Saskia's gaze actually intersected mine, and I thought she looked penitent – but out of habit, or fear, or the remains of humiliation, I turned away.

In my bed now, I sighed. Frustration and anguish fisted, again, in my stomach.

I'd seen several signs posted for the Unity Service meeting at which they were going to discuss some memorial project in Daniel's honour. It was tomorrow. Could I just show up? It had said *All welcome.* They couldn't throw me out, surely?

Maybe Saskia and the others just needed to be sure of my sincerity and desire to change.

My eyes burned. I tried closing them. I longed for sleep.

It wasn't that I wasn't tired. But my brain wouldn't stop, wouldn't stop, wouldn't stop. It was already revving up even more. At lunch with the burnouts, Gail Manuel and Wendell Butler had been talking about how getting high relaxed them, helped them sleep. I was envious.

I needed air. I pushed back the quilt and got dressed rapidly: baggy old jeans, my biggest sweatshirt, warm wool socks, thick boots. Around my neck I wound an ancient grey knitted scarf that had belonged to Daniel (before Saskia gifted him with a cashmere one). Then I grabbed my coat and quietly slipped out into the hall and down the dorm stairs.

Of course no one was supposed to leave the dorm after curfew, but our housemother, Mrs Kingston, was old, and so long as you were careful in the front entryway, it was fairly easy to get past her apartment's perpetually ajar door.

I had no trouble. Soon I was outside and pulling on my mittens.

It wasn't difficult to see my way, the campus was thoroughly covered with lighting and the moon was full. Snow crunched beneath my feet as I headed across the girls' residential quad. There was a wooded area not too far away with a little-known path that took you from Pettengill to Lattimore. It was a place Daniel had liked, and it would be pretty there now in the snow and moonlight. It would feel, perhaps, like I was somewhere else. Somewhere far away. Hokkaido in winter, perhaps. That was where my mother had grown up. I had seen pictures of it.

"Have you – are you – what about Mother?" I had said to my

father. It was the morning of Daniel's funeral. It had taken me that long to bring it up. To debate internally about calling her myself and realise that I couldn't. Couldn't. Unbelievable. But that was my family. Our family. My family.

We were at the kitchen table, not eating. My father's hands were cupped round his coffee mug. He was watching the liquid inside as if floating on its surface were some code he might decipher if he squinted hard enough. He said, "I called her. I told her."

I thought I heard Bubbe snort. I ignored her. Something in me went very still. "Then is she—"

He interrupted me, speaking rapidly. "It's too far for her to come, Frances. She's upset. Of course she's upset, in her way. But it would do no good for her to come. It wouldn't change anything. We – that's over, Frances. It's just... it's over. It's been over. Sayoko's not—" He stopped. Then, strongly: "She can't come."

And in my inner ear I heard Daniel whisper: *She has found delight in freedom from attachment.*

I don't know what I felt then. I tried to see my father's expression, but he was holding up his mug before his face. And so after a minute I simply said, "Oh." Because I had trained myself: no scenes. No drama.

I hadn't believed it, though. I couldn't believe it. And so I'd taken a deep breath and emailed. Three times I emailed her, at the general address for the monastery – hating that there was no privacy – and then, finally, she emailed back with another Buddhist quote.

Everything is always changing.

She had added *I love you, Frances,* but that hadn't mattered. It was like getting a reply from Daniel's book of aphorisms, except Sayoko was serious. She loved no one, it was clear – except Buddha and the hope of enlightenment. My hands had actually been shaking as I deleted the email.

I was not enlightened.

Suddenly breathing hard, I plunged into the little wood. A couple of other people had been here before me; the imprint of their footprints glittered on the narrow path in the recent snow. I deliberately stamped my feet into the snowy crust where the other prints weren't, leaving a distinct trail of my own passing. Left. Right. Left. It was oddly satisfying.

But then I noticed how pathetically small my footprints were. Anyone coming up this path would think they had been made by a child. Would smile at the thought. Would perhaps imagine a cute little girl in a pink snowsuit, happy, delighting in winter.

The idea infuriated me. I could kick the path clear of snow, I thought. I could stomp up and down until it was trampled flat, until I had destroyed the big footprints, until the only path here was the one I had made. No sooner had I had the thought than I began to execute it. With the side of my boot I swept sideways at the crust of snow on the path. I jumped up and down to destroy the larger footprints. With my head down, I went furiously forward, crunching, stomping, jumping, flailing, sweeping, kicking.

I don't know why I looked up.

There were two figures just ahead. Even in the moonlit dark,

I could see that they were bulky figures with shoulders. Men. Not boys, not students. One was seated on a large rock, the other leaned against a tree trunk. There was something stealthy about their appearance. Until they heard me, they had clearly been deep in conversation. But at my noisy approach, their heads lifted quickly and turned towards me. And although I couldn't see their features or expressions, I didn't need to. They were looking straight at me, and they were not pleased at being interrupted.

What I did next was stupid. But I couldn't help it.

Instinctively I turned and ran.

6

Even for the tall, strong, and athletically fit, I wouldn't recommend running through the snow at night in heavy boots. For me it was pure disaster within thirty strides. No sooner had I emerged from the wooded area back on to the well-lit grounds of Pettengill than my left foot struck something beneath the snow and I went sprawling on to my hands and knees.

I screamed. And while I fell, somehow I had enough time for the flashing thought that Saskia wouldn't have tripped, wouldn't have fallen.

She wouldn't have been out alone at night either.

I had lost my right mitten; my fingers were bare and icy, clutching snow. There was a dull roaring in my ears – my own inner panic. Frantically I began to clamber to my feet.

And then a pair of arms grabbed me at the waist and assisted me the rest of the way upright. Worried eyes peered down. "Frances? Are you OK? I didn't mean to scare you, back in the woods. It's the middle of the night! What are you doing out here?"

I blinked, astonished at being towered over, held, and yet

apparently unthreatened. After a second or two the face and voice and words all came together in familiarity and began to make sense. James Droussian, post-grad student and drug dealer, frowning at me in what appeared to be genuine concern and breathing perfectly normally, just as if he hadn't been running after me. The contrast with my own laboured panting was very obvious.

Apparently I had not after all been in mortal danger.

"Are you OK? Frances?"

My knees hurt. So did the heels of both hands. And so did the mysterious organs of humiliation, located in invisible pouches just below each eye and in the centre of the throat.

"Yeah," I managed.

I found my gaze drifting beyond James, towards the woods. I saw no one else there, or anywhere around. It had obviously been James I'd just seen in the woods, even though he was a boy, not a man. My mistake, in the dark. Had the other figure been a boy too? Another Pettengill student? Somehow it didn't seem possible; there had been something so mature about the stance – well, I'd thought that instantly of both figures, and been wrong. One had been James. Still... what had they been doing? At this hour? Something about how they looked had panicked me...

"Frances? Say something. Anything. You're really OK?"

"Yes," I said absently to James as I still watched the edge of the woods. "I'm fine. Thanks." Then I gathered myself and looked straight up at him. "But what are *you* doing out here? It's got to be four in the morning! And who was that with you in the woods just now?" The words spilled out quickly, suspiciously. I didn't care. His behaviour *was* suspicious. What was he up to? Middle of the night drug deals? I put my hands on my hips. "Well?" I said defiantly. "Why did you chase me like that?"

James reached into a pocket and withdrew something. Grinning, he dangled it above my nose. "To give you back your mitten."

I felt myself blush. I snatched the mitten but didn't back down. "What are you doing out here?"

He countered, easily, "Stuff. How about you?"

"I couldn't sleep. I needed some air."

James nodded. "Stuff of your own, huh?" Then in some subtle way his body shifted, and even in the dark he looked somehow... cheerful. Cheerful and *dumb*. "So hey, can I walk you back to your dorm?" James asked. "Maybe you can, you know, still get an hour or two of sleep." In a curiously graceful, courtly gesture, he offered an arm.

I didn't move. James probably was dumb. Why else would anyone deliberately do an extra year of high school? You had to be either dumb or insane. Although James might have business reasons for staying in high school. No better clients than a bunch of rich preppies, after all.

Daniel hadn't been a rich preppy. Again I wondered, how had he afforded his drug habit?

Focus. I had to focus. "James, you didn't say who that was with you," I repeated. "Or what you were doing."

He gave me that smile of his, but this time I didn't feel

charmed. He said cheerily, "I'm not answering those questions, little Frances. It's business, OK?"

Business. Little Frances.

In my mind's eye I could see Daniel again. No. Not Daniel. Daniel's corpse.

James was still offering me his arm. His face was all dumb concern again. Or still. I wasn't sure. I found I had taken his arm. I allowed him to guide me back towards Pettengill. Suddenly, intensely, I knew that whoever was back there in the woods, whoever it was that I had glimpsed was someone I did not want to meet.

Business.

And then the organs of humiliation pulsed. They pushed against my tear ducts. Business. James's dumb grin. Grinning, while my brother was dead.

James was talking. "Seriously, you should've seen yourself. You came along, stomping the ground like you thought you were the Fee Fie Foe Giant. Then you took one look at us and ran like Bambi. It was pretty hilarious."

Hilarious. He was going on. On and on...

"Shut up," I whispered fiercely. Then I screamed it. "Shut up! Shut up!"

I could feel James's surprise. I didn't look at him. I wanted to say it again but I didn't have the extra breath. I found I was already using everything I had.

"Hey," James was saying. "Hey, Frances." Still holding my arm, he stopped walking and swung round to face me. I stopped too. We had reached the main part of campus. The lighting was stronger, and I could see James's expression clearly. "I'm sorry," he said gently. "I didn't mean to be rude. I understand you're upset. You have a right. You've had a tough time. I was trying to, um, to distract you."

"Distract me." I discovered that, after all, I had plenty of breath. Rage consumed me. I wasn't afraid of James Droussian, no matter how many Evil Drug Distribution Men he hung out with in the woods.

James was still looking down at me. Then he said earnestly, "I've thought about Daniel a lot."

"Oh, really?" I said. "Why would that be? Let me think. Could it be that Daniel was a good customer of yours? Are you feeling guilty?"

"Frances, Daniel and I got high together a couple of times, no big deal, but that was all—"

"Business," I mimicked recklessly. "Just business. Is that what you tell yourself?"

James tugged at his ponytail. "Frances, I swear to you, I never sold Daniel smack. I *swear*. I had nothing to do with—"

"Right," I said. "Sure. Whatever you say."

I began marching across the quad alone. I felt James fall into step beside me again, loping easily while I was moving as rapidly as I could without running. This would probably make a funny cartoon too. Bambi and the Fee Fie Foe Giant. Ha. But wait – why did I care? So what if James Droussian found me funny? Who cared? What was wrong with me?

"Believe me, I would never sell smack," James was insisting. "Some things are OK, you know, but others—"

I couldn't leave that alone. I stopped again. "Oh, you have *principles*. You make *distinctions*. Isn't that nice? I feel much better."

"Listen, Frances, Daniel was responsible for his own actions. Just like you're responsible for yours. And I am for mine."

"Whose stupid philosophy is that? Cain's?"

"Huh?" James couldn't follow me.

"You remember Cain," I said rapidly. "Brother of Abel. Killer of Abel. 'I am not my brother's keeper.' That's your philosophy. That's what you're saying."

James's forehead furrowed. "What?" He bent down to look solemnly into my eyes. "No, I'm not. He wasn't my brother. Frances, what are *you* trying to say? That *you* feel responsible for Daniel's death?"

My jaw dropped. For a second I just gaped. Idiot! How dare he? James Droussian wasn't even someone who could be respected.

I slapped him.

7

If only I could be invisible. That lingering fantasy from child-hood swept over me the next afternoon as I crossed the main Pettengill quad to the stark New England Congregational chapel where Unity Service conducted their meetings. I'd only ever come to the chapel for large assemblies, during which the building's main entrance was thrown open, so this time the weight of the heavy wooden double doors was a surprise to me. I pulled hard at one of them. The door shifted a few unwilling inches, and I was able to slip inside before it thudded shut. I felt I'd barely escaped being crushed.

For some reason I thought of James Droussian and the dumbfounded yet knowing look on his face after I'd slapped him early that morning. A feeble wash of renewed anger stirred inside me. Somehow it strengthened me a little.

Right now I had the exact same feeling in my stomach that I'd had the one time I'd made myself go to a school dance. Daniel and I had both been freshmen.

Are you going? I'd asked Daniel, trying not to sound

desperate, trying not to sound scared. *Will you hang out with me if I come?*

Sure. Don't be an idiot. There'll be people to talk to. It'll be fine, Frances.

But it hadn't been fine. I was dressed all wrong, I couldn't think of anything to say to anyone. And then Saskia had come over to Daniel as he stood a little apart from me, and she'd smiled shyly, and I'd noticed her hair had got longer, and she wasn't wearing her glasses any more... and she'd asked Daniel if he wanted to dance, and he'd said *Yes.*

For a moment I thought again of not attending the Unity meeting. I was already late; I'd dithered so much about coming. I could still return to my room – my safe room with its satisfying, dark paintings. But then I remembered what else was now on the wall of my room. The mirror with its drape of black silk. The mirror that said: *You owe your brother.* The mirror that said: *You were so wrong about everything.*

I marched myself towards the meeting room.

Almost at once I heard several voices clearly. I peered into the room and saw a clump of Unity Service people in a large circle of folding chairs. They were intent on one another; no one noticed me at first as I lingered just outside the door with my doubts. But then Wallace Chan looked up. "Frances!" He sounded shocked.

Everyone stopped talking. People turned towards me. Everyone stared. Their faces all blurred together and for a few seconds I couldn't have put a name to any of them.

I stood in the doorway. I couldn't move.

Then I heard a wonderful familiar voice saying my name. Ms Wiles, my art teacher, was there in front of me. I was surprised to see her, and then relieved. "Come sit with me," she said. "We're just getting started."

My lips moved in the semblance of a smile. I settled uneasily on the edge of the chair beside her. At least Saskia was a few chairs away. "Hi," I said to the air, aware that I sounded dreadfully shy and unsure. I slid my backpack to the floor. I thought about at least unwinding Daniel's scarf; everyone else had taken off their outdoor things. But I didn't.

As the awkward silence continued, I looked covertly round the circle. Besides Saskia and Wallace, I noticed Patrick Leyden. A few teachers, the associate dean. And lots of students: George de Witt, Julie Binell, Jim Amara, a couple of other Lattimore-scholarship students, José Lamas and Pammy Rosenfeld. Eric Zhu. Robert Jenkins. Allysa Axelband. A freshman. No idea. Jenny Rubin. Mandy Somebody. James—

James! To my knowledge he wasn't a Unity member. What was he doing here? His chair was pushed slightly back and out of perfect alignment with the circle. I felt personally affronted by his presence. I hurried my eyes past him. Margaux Burnett. No idea. Sean Van Dorpe. Mahmoud Hassona. Laurel Boylan. Nicole Ruffine. I gave up on names and just counted. Twenty-nine.

No, thirty. Andy Jankowski was not part of the circle, but sat against the wall on the other side from where I was. He smiled tentatively at me, and I found myself smiling back. I straightened in my chair.

I looked at Saskia. She was looking at Patrick Leyden. Patrick

Leyden, God's gift to Pettengill. Saskia seemed to be asking a question with her expression.

Then she looked again at me, and Ms Wiles put an encouraging hand on my arm.

I bit my lip. *Please*, I prayed silently, though I wasn't entirely sure what I was praying for. Not to be kicked out? Not to be humiliated? My eyes met Saskia's. I don't know what she read there. She looked again towards Patrick Leyden. Then she said hurriedly, "Welcome, Frances. Just to catch you up. We want to do something – select a special project – to memorialise Daniel."

Air returned to the room.

Saskia went on more calmly. "Let me go over the top ideas, and we can discuss them as a group. Then we'll have a straw vote, after which the officers will meet with Mr Leyden." All the heads in the circle moved as one to look at Patrick Leyden, who simply waved a hand, as if he were the President coming off *Air Force One*. After allowing the moment of adulation, he nodded at Saskia, and she continued. "After that, we'll come back with a decision, oh, within a day or so, and get started on implementation."

My stomach had begun to roil again. But the worst was over, surely? I watched my hands in my lap. I listened to Saskia talk about a big fundraising drive. About using the money to purchase a van for the food pantry, Daniel's name to be painted on its side. Or purchasing large quantities of coats for the poor. Saskia read the suggestions and their benefits off a clipboard, and people added more pros and cons. It was all very orderly and, in its way, impressive. I felt another pang of guilt at my previous nonparticipation.

I wondered too how this all felt for Saskia. She seemed very composed, but beneath that it must have been hard for her. She and Daniel had been inseparable for two years.

When Patrick Leyden made some comment, my brain flitted off to think about how much Daniel would have loved it – that the great Leyden himself was working on a memorial for *him*. Before we started at Pettengill, Daniel had actively hunted down information on Leyden and Cognitive Reach, Leyden's successful Internet company. He'd shown me articles from *Fortune* and *Business Week* and *The Wall Street Journal*.

Think of it, Frances. Leyden flies here from New York in his private jet a couple of times a month! He's very involved with Unity. We'll probably even meet him. Isn't that incredible?

Yeah, but... don't you think he looks kind of like a rodent? I could draw him a tail. And those ears—

Daniel had turned sharply away from me, snatching the newspaper out of reach of my pencil. *Oh, grow up, Frances.*

"Are you OK?" whispered Ms Wiles. She squeezed my arm slightly.

I nodded. I forced my attention back to what Saskia was saying.

"OK, there's one more possibility, and – everyone should know – this one is actually Mr Leyden's idea. It's ambitious, but, well, I'm excited about it. And I know Daniel would approve."

There was a pause. Again I watched all the heads swivel

towards Patrick Leyden. He held the moment, seeming to enjoy it. Then he said indulgently, "Go ahead, Saskia."

For a split second before she spoke, Saskia glanced at me. Then she looked down at her clipboard and read aloud: "Education doesn't begin with high school. But by the time a kid is of high school age, he or she may already have picked up bad intellectual habits and a negative attitude about the future. This is especially true for children that come from disadvantaged backgrounds like, well, like—" She swallowed. "Like Daniel's."

I sat up in my chair. I stared at her, disbelieving. Like Daniel's? Well, and like mine! And like Saskia's, for that matter! How could she publicly say—?

She was still reading from her clipboard. "But for these children, a terrific education can still make a difference – if it begins early enough." She looked up. "So, what Mr Leyden is proposing is that we expand the concept of the Unity scholarships to younger kids. We'd start, again, right here in Lattimore. There are some parochial schools around here that aren't bad – elementary and middle schools. So: The Daniel Leventhal scholarships, endowed and in perpetuity for the kids of Lattimore."

Saskia had finished. I took a deep breath. OK. I was oversensitive and wrongheaded about the scholarships, I knew that. I listened while the circle began to applaud. When Patrick Leyden stood up, the applause continued even more strongly, until he raised a hand. They obeyed him like an orchestra obeys its conductor.

"Of course, we'd have to raise quite a lot of money for this," he said. "We'd need an ambitious capital campaign. But the fact is, we have some very wealthy alumni out there and, frankly, I have a bit of influence." He smiled. Everyone smiled back at him.

"Also," he said, "I'm thinking that now we have a high enough profile and reputation to get big donations elsewhere as well. *Huge* donations. Because this isn't just a worthy project, it's a *saleable* one, like the original Pettengill scholarships. But this time we'd be in an even better position with respect to publicity."

"The Presidential Freedom Award," someone murmured.

"Yes, that will certainly help quite a bit. *Quite* a bit. And that was my first thought. But I have just in the last few minutes had another idea that I think will garner us a lot of press as well. Frances?"

Suddenly he was looking right at me. Patrick Leyden was looking right at me. And everyone else was looking at me too.

"Frances," said Patrick Leyden pleasantly, "would you be willing to head up this capital campaign? Not really 'head up' – I'll do that, behind the scenes – but sign the fundraising letter and provide the public face of the campaign?"

I froze in my chair.

"Because the fact is, Frances, I'm hoping that this thing will really take off. Just the same as it did with the high school scholarships. And we'd have Unity scholarships at private middle and elementary schools all over the country, not just here in Lattimore. It *could* happen, if we have the right media hook – and Frances, *your* name, *your* story about Daniel, could make that vital difference. Could be that explosive media hook."

I felt everyone's eyes on me.

"Frances Leventhal," Patrick Leyden continued pompously, "this is your chance. You can lead our campaign in your brother's name, for the sake of all those kids who, like him, could have been saved by earlier exposure to more of life's, well, possibilities."

I couldn't look away from Patrick Leyden's big bobbling earlobes. I opened my mouth to speak, but nothing came out. Finally I managed to look desperately over at Ms Wiles. *Help*, I thought. *Help me.*

She smiled. "What an opportunity, Frances!"

At that moment James Droussian spoke. "Come on, Mr Leyden," he drawled. "That's, like, vampiric. You can't expect Frances to diss her brother publicly."

Stark silence again in the room.

Then: "Vampiric?" said Patrick Leyden.

James stood up. He faced Patrick Leyden across five yards of the circle. "Yeah. You know, like a vampire."

"I am aware," said Patrick Leyden, "of the definition."

"Well, then," said James, "you understand that—"

Next to me, Ms Wiles said sharply, "Both of you, stop it. I think Frances is capable of speaking for herself here. Frances—"

"Bull." James turned directly to Ms Wiles, who was glaring at him. "Take one look at her."

Everybody did. I couldn't help it, I cringed. My mind was swooping in dizzy circles.

"Frances—" began Ms Wiles.

"Frances looks like a kicked kitten," James interrupted. "This is just wrong. Forget it."

I thought about invisibility, about ways to disappear. I noticed that Saskia had hunched her shoulders up to ear level and was clutching her arms. Her eyes darted from Patrick Leyden to James to me and back.

Patrick Leyden took a few steps forward and stabbed a finger towards James. "Who are you? You're not a regular member of Unity!"

"My name is James Droussian. I'm a post-grad. I'm a friend of Frances's."

"Oh, get real," said Wallace Chan viciously. "You're not a friend of Frances's. No one is. And those of us who know you – well, let's just say that I can't believe you'd seriously presume to lecture us about ethics."

There was some murmuring, some movement. Then James laughed, sounding genuinely amused. "Oh, I'll presume. Believe me."

Ms Wiles had put her hand on my arm again, but somehow I didn't want to look at her. I moved so that her hand fell off.

Wallace Chan swivelled towards me. "Frances, you haven't said what you think."

An uncomfortable minute passed in which everyone looked at me. *No one is.* I heard it again and again. *No one is.*

Then George de Witt cleared his throat and said, "You know, James does have a point. Frances doesn't look comfortable, and—" He glanced nervously at Patrick Leyden. "What if we just tabled this for now and went back to the van idea? We could really use another one for the local food pantry, and we could easily raise that sort of money without Frances. Maybe we could even get several vans. Wouldn't that be great?"

Nobody else said anything and, after a moment, George visibly deflated.

Then I felt a slight touch on my shoulder. I looked at Ms Wiles, but she had half turned in her chair and was looking behind me, frowning in puzzlement.

Andy Jankowski was suddenly looming over me. With one hand he was holding his coat out to me again. Even though I was still wearing my own.

"Frances Leventhal?" he said carefully. "I would like to leave now. Would you like to leave too?"

And all at once I could talk. "Yes," I said. "Thank you."

My legs worked. They supported me as I got up. I put on Andy's coat on top of my own. I just wanted to, right then. I buttoned it, slowly and carefully, all the way to my throat. I stooped for my backpack and found that Andy already had it. "Thank you, Andy," I said. My voice sounded fine. It carried across the whole room.

The silence was thicker than oil paint. I didn't care. I walked with Andy. I didn't even look back at Ms Wiles. My footsteps, and Andy's, echoed all the way out of the room, all the way to the chapel's heavy double doors.

Andy reached out and pulled one of the doors open easily, as if it were made of rice paper.

8

After dinner that evening I sneaked away from campus and went to Bubbe's house. I don't know why I went, they weren't expecting me. Or maybe I do know. Maybe I thought I might find Daniel there. Oh, not for real, of course. But maybe I hoped I could find some memories of him there. Something to take away the feeling of that awful meeting.

Did they do it on purpose, to make me go away? Saskia had said I wasn't welcome.

"Andy?" I'd said, as Andy Jankowski and I walked, together, away from the chapel, across the snowy quadrangle.

"Yes, Frances Leventhal?"

I took a deep breath. "How – how did you know I wanted to leave that meeting?" I watched his profile closely.

The furrow deepened on Andy's brow. "They were all looking at you," he said. "They were all talking about you. Not *to* you. I learned how to leave when that happens to me." He suddenly looked very earnest and he turned towards me, though he didn't meet my eyes. "It's not hard. You can get up and go, Frances Leventhal. Nobody stops you."

With difficulty I said, "You showed me. Thanks."

We were silent some more. And then Andy said, "Also. That one boy said you didn't have any friends. I didn't like that."

I couldn't reply. My throat had closed.

Still cringing a little at the memory of my talk with Andy – and yet warmed as well – I slipped in the front door of Bubbe's house as quietly as I could. But my father heard and looked up from the shabby wing chair in the parlour, near the entry. He might have muttered hello at an inaudible level. I nodded just in case he had. At least Bubbe was nowhere to be seen, though it was impossible to enter her house without being aware of a certain baleful heaviness in the air.

"I just came by to pick something up," I improvised. My father nodded slowly. Indifferently? Open on his lap, but turned over so that it was clear he wasn't reading it right then, was an ancient hardcover copy of Stanislaw Lem's *Solaris.* I felt my lips tighten. The book was, in part, about a very lonely man. I wondered if it was helping my father somehow to reread it. I doubted it. I had read it three years ago, when I was working my way through the authors my father most admired. I was past that now, naturally.

Rapidly, feeling his eyes, his silence, I shed my coat and Daniel's scarf and reached down to tug off my wet boots. When I looked up, my father was still watching me, but his expression was blank and he didn't say anything. I straightened. My father cleared his throat. Bit his lip, for all the world as if he wanted to initiate a conversation and was finding it difficult. But nothing came out.

I knew it must be a tough time for him. He had lost his wife, his son. He wasn't a bad person, just... who he was. I wished I cared. No. No, I didn't. I didn't even care enough to try to hurt him, as I could have done easily by asking how his writing was going. That was always good for a little blood, as Daniel had often demonstrated.

I turned and went upstairs. I felt him watch me go.

I went, not to my own old room, but to Daniel's. Entering, flipping the light switch, closing the door behind me, for a moment it was almost as if my brother were still alive. I was grateful once again for Bubbe's arthritis, which kept her mostly on the main floor of the house. Otherwise she would have ruthlessly sorted through and thrown out Daniel's things.

I looked around. In a way, the room was a time warp from when Daniel was fourteen, the year we went to Pettengill. Over the ancient flowered wallpaper that Daniel had so hated were his calendar photos of naked and semi-naked women, each one meticulously affixed to the wall with tape. The one real poster was a colourful and explicit medieval crucifixion, which Daniel had purchased from a mail-order art catalogue solely to piss off Bubbe. You had a great view of Jesus's incongruously serene face when you sat on Daniel's narrow mattress, which lay directly on the bare wood floor. Also typically Daniel: the top dresser drawer had been shoved closed so carelessly that it gaped an inch at one side. Even the dust seemed normal, because no one ever cleaned in this house.

Disadvantaged backgrounds, like Daniel's.

It was sort of the truth. But it was so patronising. And how could Saskia – she came from Lattimore too! I sighed. So much for my plans to atone.

I went to the dresser and gently pulled Daniel's drawers open one by one, looking inside but not touching. Underwear, socks. His socks would probably fit me, I thought. I left them. An MIT sweatshirt, a forest green tee, even a once-beloved pair of footed pyjamas from maybe ten years ago. I closed each drawer gently, thinking of how Daniel would have slammed them.

There was a box in the corner, containing hastily packed things from Daniel's dorm room. I knelt and – feeling a kind of defensive guilt – rifled through it. Clothing, of course. Books, including some graphic novels – Daniel had had a major obsession with Neil Gaiman's Sandman books and had even, I saw on close examination, stolen a couple from the library. I pulled the library books out, wondering if I ought to return them, and noticed a small package tucked in between the side of the box and the books. Condoms.

Well. It wasn't like I hadn't known.

I put everything back in the box and closed its flaps.

I crossed to the closet and opened it. Dust bunnies on the floor, a very few things hanging from misshapen metal hangers, including a navy wool Pettengill blazer that Daniel had looked great in last winter. I felt my shoulders move a little in distaste as I looked at it. I raised my eyes upwards. On the top shelf, some old games: Monopoly, a big tub of Lego. And next to the Lego, half hidden by the tub, Mr Monkey.

Mr Monkey! I felt my mouth shape itself into a smile. So this was what I was searching for.

A small brown moulded-plastic squeeze toy covered with fake fur, Mr Monkey had accompanied Daniel everywhere when we were small and lived in Cambridge with Sayoko; a whole family. Famous family story: at the age of four Daniel had tucked Mr Monkey into an enormous teddy bear display at FAO Schwarz, and then couldn't find him again. Six store clerks had been pressed into service, ripping the display apart, while Daniel wailed and wailed. I wasn't sure if I really remembered this incident, I would have been only three years old. But I felt like I remembered. I could almost see Daniel and the teddies... and his face, transcendent, when Mr Monkey was restored to him.

I stretched up for Mr Monkey but couldn't reach it, and, too impatient to go get a chair or step stool, I jumped. On the second leap my fingertips grazed Mr Monkey, so I gave it one more try and triumphantly managed to knock the toy on to the floor.

Mr Monkey's head bounced off and rolled among the dust bunnies. I knelt and grabbed both pieces. Surely I could easily pop the head back on...

I paused. Mr Monkey's hollow body was not empty. Still on my knees, I backed out of the closet and peered more closely. A couple of small plastic bags were tucked inside the fur-covered plastic shell.

My hand was perfectly steady as I reached and pulled them out.

I breathed then. It was not cocaine. Not smack. Not uppers or downers or anything that really would have scared me. It was just pot. It was just a few ounces of marijuana in one Ziploc bag and, in the second, some cigarette papers.

It might have been there for years. It was possible. I unzipped the bag and touched the grains. I sniffed. It smelled sweet, heavy, unmistakable. I sat back on my heels. I thought about flushing it down the toilet. I thought about making muffins with it, and giving them to Bubbe. No. To Saskia, and all the Unity people. They'd catch me, though. They'd catch me, and I'd be expelled.

I might want that. I tested the thought. I whispered it out loud. "What if I were expelled?" But no, of course I didn't want that. There was nowhere else for me to go. There wasn't even a public school option in Lattimore any more.

It was still amusing, though, to imagine pretty, perfect Saskia, high. Saskia, giggling senselessly, discovered by her hero Patrick Leyden in a completely wasted state. I hated her again suddenly. I hated her, and Patrick Leyden too. I hated all of them, everyone who'd been at that meeting. Yes, even Ms Wiles! Everyone but Andy. I'd slip them all worse than marijuana if I could. They could all die horribly, as Daniel had! I'd – I'd—

And now my hands *were* shaking. I clenched them tightly over the Ziploc bag. This was a stupid, useless fantasy; the only person it was harming was me.

In my head Daniel's voice gibed. *Mental activity is the supreme suffering.* I winced.

I ought to go and flush the marijuana down the toilet right now. Or I could give it to James Droussian for resale. I hated him too, though I did recognise that he had tried to help me in the Unity Service meeting. Sort of. Maybe this would even the score. I did not want to be in his or anyone's debt. There was only one person in the entire world who I could stand right now, and he was retarded.

I found I was wiping furiously at my cheeks.

I felt humiliated. I needed – I really needed—

I looked down again at the two halves of Mr Monkey. At Daniel's Ziploc bags.

I wondered if Andy had ever got high. I wondered if he would like to try. I imagined us getting high together. It was the kind of thing you did with your friends, right? Share?

Andy might like it. I might like it. Daniel had liked it. Everybody liked it.

Around me Bubbe's house felt heavy as ever. Nobody was coming up here to Daniel's room. I could stay all night if I liked, and walk back to Pettengill in the morning for classes.

I don't remember deciding. I got up and turned off the overhead light. I turned on the smaller lamp on the floor and sat on Daniel's mattress.

I had once seen others do this, and it wasn't hard at all, rolling the cigarette paper tightly round a small amount of weed, then twisting the ends. I was quite satisfied with the result. There were matches too in Mr Monkey. Very considerate of Daniel.

He'd be laughing right now. Especially as I carefully fitted Mr Monkey back together and set him down beside me on the mattress. Then, and only then, did I lean against the wall with Daniel's pillows behind me.

I knew not to inhale too sharply, too deeply, at first.

8

I'd never even tried to get high before, so all I knew was what Daniel had said and what I had occasionally seen. I had nothing to compare my experience to. Still, waking in Daniel's room the next morning and breathing in the stale, sweet air (which lingered even though sometime in the small hours I'd forced the old window open nearly three inches), I decided that the marijuana simply hadn't had much effect on me. I had not collapsed into paroxysms of giggles. And I'd had no deep feelings of relaxation; if anything, I'd remained alert and even a little tense as I smoked first one and then a second handmade cigarette. I'd been entirely focused on accustoming myself to the smell. To the tight, hot feeling in my lungs as I figured out how to inhale, how to draw in the smoke and hold it in my lungs. How to gradually exhale. I'd felt a mild pleasure at my progress. But that was it.

Maybe it was old stuff after all. Or I was immune. Or it took a few tries.

Maybe I was relieved.

Maybe I was disappointed.

I curled on to my side on Daniel's mattress and blinked at the red neon numbers of his digital alarm clock. One good thing was that I had slept well for a few hours. I knew I ought to get up now – it was only six, but I would need to shower, wash my (no doubt) reeking hair, and put on different clothes before heading back to Pettengill. Idly I hoped there was something reasonable in my closet to wear, something warm. Of course, if the worst came to the worst, there was always Daniel's wool school blazer, hanging across the room in his closet.

I wondered if Mr Monkey would fit in the blazer's pocket. Then I forced myself to get up and head down the icy hallway towards a hot shower.

Always before, when alone, I had walked between Bubbe's house and Pettengill using the main roads. But Daniel had preferred the shortcut path through the woods, the one that went very near the spot at which, the other night, I'd encountered James Droussian and whoever it was he'd been with. This morning, defiantly, I took that route. And somehow I was not surprised to come upon James just before the woods ended and the smooth snowy grounds of the campus began.

James was sitting alone on a rock. From where I stopped, a few yards behind him, I could see his profile clearly, see the way his left cheekbone stood out in sharp contrast to the background of tree bark, see the intent way he'd drawn his brows together and was staring towards the campus.

What did I have to lose? I stepped forward. I cleared my

throat. I spoke perhaps more loudly than I normally would have. "James."

He leaped off the rock and whipped round towards me almost before the first vowel sound had left my lips. Again I felt that abrupt sense of dislocation, of things somehow wrong, that I'd felt when with him the other night. But a bare instant later as he recognised me, his body relaxed. "Frances, hey," he said affably. "Fancy seeing you here, huh? You got both mittens today?"

I nodded. I regained my own mental balance and my resolve. "I just, um, wanted to say thank you, James. For yesterday." He stared at me, his face expressionless, and I had trouble stumbling on. I did it anyway. "At the Unity Service meeting, I mean."

"Oh," said James after a second. Was his body ever so slightly tense again, or was I imagining that? "Right. No problem."

I fidgeted. There was more to say. "And I'm sorry about hitting you. I was – I'm sorry."

He didn't reply immediately. The moment stretched, and my stomach twisted, and once again I felt his words from the other night, his dumb, thoughtless words about Daniel. About me. And I felt something else too, something I didn't understand, something coming from James. I thought of the way he'd jumped up from the rock a moment ago, been suddenly in my path. I found myself swallowing.

"OK," James said finally. But his tone was even, too even, and while it should have been enough for me to hear that one word, somehow it wasn't. I didn't feel forgiven. I wasn't forgiven. I knew it.

I found myself stepping forward. "I apologise. I shouldn't have done it."

I searched James's face for forgiveness and still didn't find it. Anger flicked at me then. So the large manly drug dealer didn't care to forgive small, weak, kitten-like Frances for slapping him? Well, he could go directly to hell. I straightened my shoulders and walked past him.

"Frances."

I took another two steps before I stopped and turned. Now it was my turn to say nothing and look blank.

But James clearly wasn't impressed. And I saw now that his blankness wasn't blankness at all. It was something I recognised. Something I knew all about.

Control.

"I'm going to tell you something," James said. "And you're going to listen, and one day you're going to be grateful that I told you this, because you need to hear it. For your own safety. Are you listening?"

His voice wasn't loud. And he was standing at least five yards away from me. But I felt as constrained as if he'd been in my face, with both hands heavy on my shoulders.

I nodded like a spring-necked doll.

James said, "You believe that because you're small and female, no one will take you seriously. The other night you assumed you had the freedom to hit somebody bigger than you if you chose. You thought it was safe. I'd never hit back."

"No," I said, confused. "No, that wasn't what I was thinking—"

"Shut up," said James quietly. "I'm talking."

I shut up.

"Then you weren't thinking," he said. "Which is actually worse. In this case, you were right. I would never hit you back." And then suddenly – without rising in volume – his voice lashed out. "But I am not everybody. And your size and your sex are no guarantee of safety."

At that moment, if my brother's life had been offered to me in exchange, I couldn't have moved my eyes from James's face.

"It's a dangerous world, Frances. Don't go around thoughtlessly creating opportunities for violence. *Ever.* Because if you do, I promise you: violence *will* occur. It will come looking for you."

James didn't move a step closer. It only felt as if he had.

I stared at him. I felt my rage kicking in my gut, and my despair looking for a place to go. I was full of confusion. Why had I slapped James? It had seemed clear to me at the time. I had felt that I had to do something, make something change, or I would explode – implode—

One of Daniel's hated quotes echoed within me. *One should not use violence or have it used.*

Abruptly, the little scene was over. James brushed past me. He walked rapidly away, towards Pettengill. Still confused, uncomprehending, I watched him go.

Gradually my mind cleared. My first coherent thought was that, post-grad or not, James Droussian was definitely not dumb. And then I knew something else too.

That hadn't been a kid talking to me just now.

I *hadn't* made a mistake in the woods the other night. I had seen exactly what I'd thought I'd seen: two men. Two men, one of whom was James.

James looked young. Looked eighteen or nineteen. But he wasn't.

James Droussian – if that was his real name – was an adult.

10

A minute later I knew I had to be crazy. Daniel's death, the awfulness I felt – it was making me imagine things. Because really, what would an adult James Droussian be doing at Pettengill? Why pretend to be a teenager? To set up a prep-school drug business? Ridiculous.

However, as I trudged back towards my dorm, I allowed myself to linger on the drug business idea, because it didn't seem *entirely* ridiculous. It was impossible not to know that at least half to three-quarters of the Pettengill student body used something, sometimes. Weed and mushrooms for the burnouts. Diet pills for girls like Brenda Delahay, desperate to get or stay thin. Steroids for the jocks. Amphetamines for some of the fiercely competitive studiers. Cocaine and meths and ecstasy for the partiers. Very few people had a real problem, of course, but there was quite a lot going on, and surely it had to be lucrative for somebody. Maybe James—

But then I just shook my head. Obviously at some level there had to be adults providing all this stuff, but they certainly didn't need to be right at school, masquerading as students. There were plenty of kids ready to do the work themselves. And last year James hadn't been here, and I didn't see that his presence had changed anything. My little theory just didn't hold water. It wasn't even worth being called a theory.

Commentary from Daniel again. *The mind creates the reality, and reality creates the mind.* He'd used the aphorism mockingly, but there actually was something to this one. I was discombobulated, creating my own stupid version of reality that had nothing to do with what was real.

Feeling even more depressed than usual, I slipped back into my dorm.

I had an art class that morning, with a full two hours of clay sculpture scheduled. Normally I'd have looked forward to it, to spending time doing the one thing that made me feel entirely comfortable in my own body. Not to mention the fact that it didn't matter, in art class, if anyone wanted to talk to you or not. If you belonged or not.

But today I felt awkward. My usual eagerness to see Ms Wiles was tempered by what had happened yesterday at the Unity meeting. The fact was – I had to face it – I'd felt a little disappointed in her. I'd have thought she'd understand, immediately, what I felt when Patrick Leyden made his suggestion. In my mind's eye I could still see her face, hear her silence. James, Andy – even George de Witt, that Unity flunky – had said something to help me. But the woman I admired most in all the world had just sat there. Had said *What an opportunity!*

On purpose, then, I arrived at the art studio only after other kids had got there as well, so that there would be no opportunity for private conversation with Ms Wiles. She gave me her special encouraging smile, as always, but my own returning smile felt stiff.

Still, just breathing in the air of the studio made me feel better. I pulled the unmistakable mix of fragrances deeply into my nose and lungs and identified each of them lovingly. The wood-like perfume of the drawing boards and easels, which were always being sponged off. The plastic smell of the old yoghurt containers with their splotches of dried paint or tempera. The cold metallic tang of the sinks, mingled with a certain soapy-towel and turpentine odour. The wet-dog stench of one particular brand of watercolour paper, and the weirdly clean scent of wet clay. Finally, overlaying the whole room, the sneezy bouquet of charcoal and graphite.

For me it smelled like home.

I busied myself taking the wrappings off my fledgling sculpture. I could feel my hands simply aching to work the clay.

We were modelling a large bone – a plaster cast of an elephant's femur, to be precise. It sounded dull, but once you looked closely, once you saw how the bone flowed and changed as you walked round it, how precise and yet individual was each curve and surface and angle, you realised how extraordinary a thing it was. How impossible to replicate in clay, working in all three dimensions – infinitely more difficult than working on paper, in two. And yet how irresistible it was to try.

I squinted at the model femur, and then at my own copy. My femur was coming along, I thought. I was behind the rest of the class – the week of sitting shivah for Daniel had of course cut into all my schoolwork – but here, at least, I'd have no trouble catching up.

Ms Wiles was walking round the room, pausing at each student's shoulder to observe and make suggestions, and then raising her voice to talk more generally to the rest of the class. As I listened, as I worked, I felt myself soften towards her. She was always so fascinating.

"Working with sculpture, you can really begin to understand that making art is all about seeing clearly. Look, people. *Look.* That's the key to everything. The young Picasso was told he should break his right hand, so that he would be forced to rely more on his eyes, not on his hands. An extreme idea, but you get the point. If you don't *look,* you can't *do.*"

Earlier in the year Ms Wiles had shown us pictures of some of Picasso's work. Comparing his early paintings to his later stuff, it had been a little hard not to think that Ms Wiles was crazy. In those early pictures Picasso not only saw well, but it seemed to me that in a way he saw better than he had later, when he was so acclaimed, when he took to drawing blue cubes, to stacking facial features vertically. His early portraits were alive with realism, with accuracy. I loved them.

And yes, as Ms Wiles pointed out while showing us slides, Picasso's *Guernica* screams the agony of war – but that was emotional truth on the canvas, not physical.

I said that to Ms Wiles privately. That was the first time we'd ever talked alone; I'd crept up after class, unable to resist. "Ms Wiles? I don't really get what you were talking about."

She'd smiled at me. "Frances, is it? What didn't you get?"

"Just... about seeing. What's wrong with Picasso's early stuff? I mean, I get what you say about *Guernica*. I really do. But I'd say that *Guernica* was done with the heart, not the eyes." She'd listened so attentively that, despite myself, I found I was growing more and more passionate. "I mean, if we're going to talk about body organs. Art..." I stumbled a little, trying to explain my thoughts. "Art should be done with hands and heart, not hands and eyes. That's what *Guernica* is. Because nobody else could see what Picasso saw. Right?"

"Well," Ms Wiles said, "until he showed us all how to look." And as she smiled at me, I had a glimmer not only of what she meant, but, more importantly, of the pleasure of being able to discuss such things, seriously, with an adult who also cared about them.

I bit my lip. "Oh," I said tentatively.

"Let me show you some other artists' stuff," Ms Wiles said. "There are slides in the photography room that might make all this more clear – do you have time, or do you have to get to another class?"

I had had another class, but I hadn't cared. "Oh, yes," I'd said eagerly. "I have time."

Now, as she talked, I built up the clay base of my sculpture, then slowly walked round the plaster model trying to *see* it. What you looked at straight on wasn't what you saw when you tilted your head to the side. The shapes flowed into each other and then into something else... but it was all part of a whole. It all came together.

I went back to my own femur. I smoothed its long central line. I tried to shape the bumps of its connecting joints. I looked up at the model, down at my work. Up, down. Up, down. My hands moved.

You don't watch your hands while you work. You watch the model. Your hands work on their own. And it's best if you don't think too much about what you're doing. My mind drifted.

Seeing clearly. I thought I understood a little better now. In life I'd seen Daniel my way. I'd thought he'd been happy, but he had been unhappy enough to kill himself. If I'd looked better, I might have seen – *Guernica* in his face? Maybe?

Was that what Ms Wiles had been driving at about Picasso? If you think you already know what you're looking at, then you can't possibly see that something else is really there?

I worked on my femur. I felt its shape beneath my palms. I looked at the model, not at my clay.

Ms Wiles came up behind me, and I felt myself tighten. Under her eyes I worked the clay. I smoothed out the central bone line again. Reshaped the joint that gaped open on top. Then I stepped back and looked.

Somehow my poor femur had gone all wrong.

"Frances?" said Ms Wiles gently.

I turned.

Her voice had dropped to a level low enough that only I could hear it. "You're angry at me?"

I shrugged.

"Please don't be," Ms Wiles said. "Would you like to have tea with me later? This afternoon? My place?"

I realised in that second that I wanted nothing more. My mouth formed a real smile for her. "Oh, yes," I said. "That would be great."

11

Just before lunch time I discovered Saskia waiting for me as I left my English class. She was leaning against the wall, backpack pulling her shoulders down. When she saw me, she straightened and said my name. With one hand she lightly brushed back her hair, then it fell into place, concealing much of her face. Towering over me by inches, she peered from behind the gleaming dark curtain as a harem girl might from behind a veil. It was just the kind of thing, I knew, that drove boys crazy with lust. And she was graceful even in her preppy duck boots. In the back of my mind I wondered why it was that she didn't look ridiculous in them, especially paired with her – she had just nervously pushed back her hair again – diamond earrings. I blinked. Wait. Diamond earrings? No; they couldn't be real.

Again I was nearly overwhelmed with rage at her for being so beautiful. For having, taking, so much.

"Frances," she said again. "I just thought... I wanted to ask how you were doing. We – I feel bad about – well, you know. The Unity meeting yesterday. I don't think Patrick meant to offend you."

The corridor around us emptied as everyone rushed off towards the cafeteria for lunch. "I'm fine," I said stiffly.

Silence. Then Saskia's face hardened a little. "OK. You can't say I didn't warn you that—"

I interrupted. "You warned me I wouldn't be welcome." The walls bounced my voice around. I lowered it. "I just want to know one thing," I said rapidly. "You supposedly loved Daniel. Anyway, you fucked him." I thought Saskia's eyes widened in shock or anger, but with all the hair, I couldn't be sure. And I didn't care.

I said, "So, is that how *you* want to remember him, as some hopeless overdosing drug addict from a 'disadvantaged background'? Is that what *you* think the truth is? Or don't you care, so long as you can please Patrick Leyden?"

I stopped, a little horrified at myself. I hadn't even known those words were in me, much less about to emerge. But I also felt exhilaration, as if I'd hurled a rock at a window. The window hadn't shattered, though, and I wanted it to.

"Well?" I goaded. "I did notice one thing at that meeting, and that was how you wouldn't say boo without first looking at Leyden to make sure it was OK. Like some little flunky slave girl. And—"

Saskia cracked. She reached out quickly, forcefully, with both hands and shoved me. I stumbled and nearly fell before I caught the wall.

"You ignorant bitch," Saskia said. She turned away. Her boots stomped down the corridor. I listened to them as she disappeared from view around a corner.

Half of me wanted to run after her and apologise. The other

half was stronger, though. That half meant what it had said. That half wanted her to be in pain.

The wrong-doer suffers, Daniel mocked. *He is tormented to see his own depraved behaviour.*

I slumped.

After that, even though my feet took me automatically to the cafeteria, I realised as soon as I got there that I couldn't possibly swallow anything. Still, I found myself looking around for James Droussian. *Don't create opportunities for violence.* What would James think of the scene just past? Who had created the opportunity, Saskia or me?

My eyes skimmed past a table of jocks, then one or two of nerds, before I spotted James, stuffing fries into his mouth as rapidly as possible while listening to Margaux Burnett. Seeing him like that confirmed to me that I *had* been nuts before. Most definitely James was not an adult. Which, I realised, meant that there must have been violence in James's young life that had taught him what he knew about it.

I suddenly longed to know what that might have been. But why would James tell me anything? I was no one to him. I spun round and barrelled through two sets of double doors, out on to the snow-covered campus.

I felt a little better once in motion. I sped up to a trot, almost a run, heading more or less randomly across campus.

Ten minutes later I recognised Andy Jankowski outside the science building. He was working on the far side of the wide steps, methodically attacking the remaining ice with a metal spade.

My feet slowed and then stopped. My mouth shaped itself into an involuntary smile. "Hey, Andy."

He looked up, recognised me, and after a second moved his arm awkwardly in a wave before turning back to his work.

I went up the steps. "How are you today?" Ridiculous, I thought, that the entire width of the steps needed to be salted and cleared, when only the middle portion was really used. It just made extra work for Andy. For an instant I wondered if I could help, but Andy was nearly done.

"Good," he said. The edge of his spade smashed the surface of the last expanse of salted ice. He had astonishing physical competence. I watched as he carefully cleared every last bit of ice off the steps. Then, as if it had taken all that while to find the right words, he said, "How are you, Frances Leventhal?"

There was the usual rote quality to Andy's voice. But he looked at me quietly and waited, and somehow I couldn't just say, automatically, "OK." I bit my lip. What was it about Andy that made me want to talk? "Not good," I blurted.

Andy didn't say anything.

"I really miss my brother," I said. "I don't know what to do. I thought maybe I could help Unity with the memorial project, but – well, you know. Yesterday. And just now, I – well, anyway." I stopped. I ducked my head for an instant and then looked back up and shrugged.

Andy lifted the spade and gestured to the bag of salt. "I need to take these inside now, Frances Leventhal. I'm done with these steps."

"I'll help," I said. I tried to reach for the spade but Andy shook his head and held it out of my reach. He wouldn't let me lift the bag of salt either. Uninvited, I trailed him while he carried them inside the building. He stored everything meticulously in a big utility closet, and then swept some stray salt into a dustpan. He made no mention of what I had said, just didn't respond. I was relieved. And, somehow, calmed. All at once I realised that I wasn't alone, really. I was having tea with Ms Wiles in a few hours.

"What do you have to do next?" I asked Andy conversationally.

"Go to the gym."

"More ice to clear?"

"Yes."

"Oh," I said. And then, impulsively: "Can I come? I could help."

"No," said Andy, his expression suddenly anxious. "You can't help, Frances Leventhal. There are rules."

"Oh," I said again. "But – well, can I come just to keep you company?"

"I guess so," Andy answered after a moment. He looked puzzled but said nothing more. He closed up the utility closet, and we began to walk together in silence across the campus to the gym. Andy walked slowly, deliberately, and it was easy for me to stay in step with him.

My feeling of calm grew as we walked, until I was able to say, "Andy? May I ask you a question?"

"Yes."

"Why were you at that Unity meeting yesterday? Are you – do you—" I stumbled, trying to formulate the question. I'd wondered if Andy was one of the recipients of Unity charity, like me. But somehow I couldn't find a way to ask.

As it turned out, I didn't need to. "I work at the Unity food pantry," Andy said simply. "Two afternoons a week. They pay two whole dollars more than minimum wage." He nodded emphatically. "It's true. They do."

I found myself wondering how much Andy was paid by Pettengill. I guessed his on-campus apartment came with the job, and cafeteria meals too. "Highly skilled" and "gifted" were the words always used to describe Andy's work with trees and shrubs. "Pettengill is lucky to have him," they said. But if Andy was well paid, why would he know exactly what the minimum wage was?

"I saw the poster and thought it was a work meeting that I had to go to," Andy continued meticulously. "But it wasn't."

"I get it," I said.

But Andy wasn't done. He added matter-of-factly, "There's never real work for me to do at the pantry, Frances Leventhal. Only pretend work. But I go there and pretend anyway." He shrugged. "They pay me."

"Huh?" I said. "What do you mean, pretend work?" I had only the vaguest idea of what was done at the Unity pantry. "Don't you pack up clothes and food and stuff?"

"No." Andy's voice rose. "They have me watch the door."

"Oh," I said uncomfortably. I understood. They'd made up a job for Andy. I glanced at his face. He was scowling, watching his feet as he walked beside me. I felt renewed anger at Unity, at Saskia, at all of them. Charity was their business, so couldn't they understand how demeaning this particular plan was for Andy? He was competent at his job at Pettengill – surely he was fully capable of hauling and packing and sorting, or whatever it was that was needed at the Unity food pantry.

Then I sighed. Because it wasn't as if I were doing any better. It wasn't as if I were helping anyone with anything.

I'm ashamed of my own sister, Daniel had said.

We had reached the gym. Andy hunched his shoulders as he moved towards the entrance. "Well," I said, "if you really don't think I can help—"

"Those people think I don't notice," Andy burst out, and jerked open the gym doors. "They keep all the real work for themselves. But I'm not that stupid. And it's boring, watching the door." We stepped inside the gym.

I didn't know what to do, how to comfort him. Finally I reached out and put my hand on his coat sleeve. "I'm sorry," I said feebly. "I don't know what they're thinking. Of course you can do real work. You do it all the time here at Pettengill."

"That's right. I do!"

"That's right. But you said they pay well, at least."

"Yes." Andy stopped scowling. "Two dollars an hour more than minimum wage, Frances Leventhal. That's something."

"Yes," I said. "I guess it is."

Another moment passed, and then: "Oh, well," said Andy philosophically. "I have real work to do here." He smiled at me, and though he still looked a little sad, I was relieved to see he seemed to know how to cope with it. "I need to work now, Frances Leventhal. You can't help. You go away." He opened another utility closet and took out a shovel and a bag of salt.

"OK," I said. "I'll see you around."

"Goodbye, Frances Leventhal."

I trudged away.

12

Ms Wiles's on-campus apartment was part of a little cluster of small, cottage-like faculty homes located behind the science building, a seven- or eight-minute walk from my dorm. She had a charming little white cottage all to herself.

It was dusk now, with dark drawing on fast. I arrived at Ms Wiles's door ten minutes earlier than I should have, and when I knocked, there was no answer. Her windows were dark. I sat down on a nearby bench, hunched into my coat, and hoped she wouldn't be long.

Already the campus lighting was on. As I sat on my bench, I watched a couple of other faculty members let themselves into cottages. A little further away I saw Andy Jankowski enter a small garage; a minute later, lights went on in the windows of the eaves, and I realised that his apartment must be located there, built into the loft storey. I watched his silhouette as he pulled down the shades in each window one by one.

Like a glass held beneath an open tap, I felt myself fill slowly, inexorably, with sadness. With thoughts of Daniel. I held my arms and hunched over a little. I closed my eyes. Suicide. How could I not have known?

We had even talked about suicide once, Daniel and I.

In one of my father's early science fiction novels – written before his prose style got so convoluted that it was almost impossible to read – he had created a religious oracle who lived in seclusion. Very rarely, the oracle would be visited by a pilgrim with a desperate question. I say desperate because, if the oracle chose to answer, the price for the questioner was instant death.

Think about it, I'd said to Daniel after making him read the relevant passages. I'd wanted to talk about the book's ideas, but I certainly wasn't going to ask my father. *You'd be deciding that sometimes pure knowledge, just in the abstract, is more important than your own life.*

Is that what our dear parent says in the book? He's full of it. You could have other reasons, even stupid ones, to go talk to this oracle.

Like what? I was a little indignant. After all, I'd read the entire book, and Daniel hadn't.

Curiosity. Plain curiosity about something.

Oh, really? You'd choose to die just because you were curious?

Curiosity killed the cat. Hey, I don't know. Some people will do just about anything out of curiosity. He laughed as I made a face. *OK, not you, Frances.*

Not anyone! Not if you knew, knew for sure, that it would kill you.

Daniel shrugged, not really caring. *Frances, you're forgetting that some people can't control themselves. But all right then. What about suicide?*

Huh?

What if you went to visit this oracle because you didn't want to live anyway? You're picking death, not knowledge. You just don't have the guts to do it yourself, or maybe you figure you might as well get some big answer on the way out.

I was silenced. It was plausible. More than plausible.

Gotcha. Daniel tossed the book back at me.

I'd caught it and gone away, brooding. And now I wondered, bitterly, if Daniel had got any big answers on his way out. I would never know. I put my mittened hands to my cheeks.

And then, out of some animal instinct, I opened my eyes and sat up straight.

"Frances!" Ms Wiles said. "Hello!" She was standing before me, holding her keys in one gloved hand and a bag of groceries in the other. "You must be freezing! I'm so sorry I'm late – there was a longer line at the store than I'd expected."

I stood up hastily. "I was early," I said apologetically.

"Come in," she said. "I bought us a lemon poppy seed cake."

"Yum," I answered, following her gratefully into the warmth.

I had been in Ms Wiles's cottage three or four times, but I always needed to look around and admire it all over again. It was small, yes; just a combined kitchen and living room, a tiny bathroom and bedroom, and a heated sun porch that she used as her art studio and that, unfortunately, had always been closed off when I visited. ("I'm sorry, Frances. I've never been comfortable showing my works in progress.") But despite – or maybe partly because of – its size, Ms Wiles had managed to make the cottage so vivid.

She had painted the living-room walls a deep rose, the

bedroom was cameo blue. Most of her eclectic collection of wooden furniture ("nearly all scavenged off the street") was painted white so that all the pieces looked intentional together. She had simply thrown loose fabric over the sofa and her ancient overstuffed chair. ("Lovely material? You think? Oh, I'm laughing – the one on the chair where you're sitting is just a sheet from Kmart!")

And, she had such great *things*. She owned a sparkly turquoise floor lamp made from an old-fashioned, wheeled hair dryer, and a clock fashioned from a hubcap. ("My college lover was good at that kind of thing. Would you believe he's in advertising now? Every now and again I see one of his commercials on TV. What a bloody waste.") One whole wall was sturdy cement-block and pine-board shelving, crammed with wonderful art books ("It's a terrible weakness of mine; they're all so expensive,") and a very few lovely curios. On the walls she had hung many black-and-white photographs of old people. ("No, they're not family. I have no idea who any of them are. I buy them in antique shops.") Finally, she had an actual sterling silver tea set, the creamer of which I had noticed her caressing fondly the first time she invited me over for tea. ("Oh, you caught me. But I can't help it. I love this tea set.")

Tonight I sat on the edge of her overstuffed chair, teacup and saucer in hand, and took it all in like super-oxygenated air. It was all so civilised, so wonderful. I wanted to grow up and live in a place like this. No; I wanted it to happen immediately.

"Feeling a little more relaxed now?" said Ms Wiles sympathetically.

"Yes," I answered. And it was true. I smiled at her. "This is such good tea," I said, knowing it would please her. "What kind is it?"

"It's called Blue Sapphire. It's a special blend from the Ritz-Carlton in Boston. *They* know how to do a high tea."

"Umm," I said, sipping.

We drank our tea and ate our lemon poppy seed cake and talked about regular stuff for a few minutes. Then Ms Wiles leaned forward and asked, "How *are* you, Frances?" Which was the awful question, of course, the one to which there was really no answer. But I didn't mind it from Ms Wiles.

"I'm doing all right," I said. I looked straight at her, and she looked straight back, and after a couple of seconds I had to look down at my tea.

"Frances?" she said tentatively. "Listen, please. Yesterday at the Unity meeting – I think you misinterpreted things. No one wanted to hurt your feelings about your brother. That boy – what's that boy's name? James Something? Anyway, he—"

"Droussian," I interrupted. "James Droussian." It came out a little accusingly.

Ms Wiles shrugged. "Well, he's not one of my students. How should I know what his name is?" She frowned. "Or care. I hear things about that boy, Frances. You shouldn't go by his interpretation of things. No – no vampirism was meant. And no insult."

"I wasn't going by James's interpretation!" I was indignant. "I can take offence for myself." I paused. It was unexpectedly difficult to defend my feelings about yesterday's meeting in Ms Wiles's presence, and against her opinion. "And – and I *did* take offence."

"I see," said Ms Wiles, and took a tiny sip of her tea.

"On my own," I said.

"Uh-huh."

"I *did*! Why would you think I'd be influenced by James? I hardly know him!"

"Well. He's a handsome young man." She was suddenly studying my face.

"So what?"

"I just – never mind."

"What?"

"More tea?"

"*What?*"

Ms Wiles sat back fully on the sofa. Her expression was grave. "I just happened to notice how you were looking at him yesterday. It's no wonder, Frances. And it's nothing to be ashamed of either. We're all human, and he is very—"

"I was *not* looking at James any particular way! He – he's a goddamned drug dealer!"

My voice had gone shrill. My words sat in the air between me and Ms Wiles. They could not be taken back.

"Well," said Ms Wiles finally. "That's the rumour I'd heard. Frances, do you have proof? Of the kind I could take to the administration?"

Alarm seized me. I busied myself taking another slice of cake. "No," I said. Which was true. James had never sold anything to me. "I've just heard rumours."

"Oh."

"And I'm not influenced by him."

"I'm glad."

"And I don't understand why you would even think that. I'm not the kind of person who can't decide things for herself." Then I added, "Am I? I mean, do you think that about me?"

Silence. And then: "Would you look at me for a moment, Frances?"

I didn't. I couldn't. I picked up a crumb of cake with the tip of my index finger and put it in my mouth, and then felt my cheeks get hot. It wasn't the kind of thing you did in public – at tea. Unless, of course, you came from a "disadvantaged background".

I hadn't needed James to tell me that my brother and I were being dissed. It had just been reassuring to know I wasn't the only one who saw it.

"Please look at me, Frances."

I did, finally. Ms Wiles had beautiful eyes, long-lashed, grey. Usually their expression was playful or ironic; right now, they were filled with so much kindness that it was all I could do not to cry.

She said gently, "You're very vulnerable right now. You lost your brother in terrible circumstances. And we haven't talked about it, but I know your mum left, and you aren't close to your dad."

I didn't say anything.

"It seemed natural that you might be looking for a boyfriend right now. That's all. It's not such a bad idea, in general. With the right person. So I just wondered if that was what was going on with James, uh, Druggian. That's all."

I knew Ms Wiles hadn't forgotten James's name this time. She was trying to make me smile.

I tried. I tried, even though my head was suddenly swimming. *Looking for a boyfriend... vulnerable right now... how you were looking at him yesterday... don't create opportunities for violence... cultivate mindfulness...*

"Sweetheart," Ms Wiles said earnestly. "Frances. This is what I really wanted to say to you. Think again about participating in this project for Daniel. About being a little bit involved with Unity. I know Patrick Leyden, and I promise, he wouldn't have suggested this fundraising project if he didn't believe it could do a lot of good.

"And I know you, Frances. Better than you might guess. So trust me to know what's best for you now. I can talk to some of the kids – smooth things a little for you. Being involved with Unity, doing good things, could do *you* a lot of good."

Wasn't that what I had thought too? Until the meeting yesterday. It was what I had thought myself. I owed Daniel. I owed his memory.

"So, will you promise me to at least think about it?" Ms Wiles said. "I'm sure, if you talked to Patrick – or I could talk to him for you – I'm sure you could still take part. You wouldn't have to do anything you didn't want to do. But you would still be, well, participating."

Participating.

We wouldn't have you even if you begged to join.

"Tell me you'll think about it, Frances. Give it a couple of days' thought."

Ms Wiles waited.

"OK," I said. "I'll think about it. I'll let you know." I meant it. I was pretty sure I meant it. I just felt a little confused.

Looking for a boyfriend... not such a bad idea... he's a handsome young man...

Poor freaky kid.

"That's settled, then," said Ms Wiles. "We'll talk about it again in a few days. Now: more tea?" She smiled at me.

"No, thanks. I'd better be going." *You can get up and go. Nobody stops you.*

"Are you sure?"

"Yes, I am. Thanks for the tea. And for everything."

"You're welcome, Frances," she said, and escorted me to the door of her wonderful cottage. "You're welcome anytime."

I went out into the cold.

13

That night I fell asleep at long last only to drop into a weird dream. From the doorway of Bubbe's living room I was watching my father, hunched over one of his legal pads, writing. Bubbe materialised beside me and hissed in my ear: *Pretend work! Pretend work!* And then my father dropped his legal pad and curled into a ball, and suddenly he wasn't my father at all. He was Daniel, and he was on the floor of a big empty building that I somehow knew was the old Leventhal shoe factory. He was dead, and Saskia was sitting cross-legged beside him. Then, sensing my presence, she looked up. She extended an open hand towards me. In the centre of her palm sat a tiny statue of Buddha, holding the plump bag that signified wealth. Saskia's eyes glowed red like a demon's, but her cheeks were wet.

I woke up, turned on the light, and checked the clock. I had slept barely twenty minutes. The night stretched ahead.

At dinner I'd spotted James across the cafeteria and felt myself blush, thinking of what Ms Wiles had said. She was completely wrong, of course. I'd turned away, only to see Saskia and George de Witt. Saskia's face was intense as she leaned closer to George. Rapidly and of their own accord my feet moved to a small out-of-the-way table, where I sat by myself, my back to the room, and read the same page of my history textbook over and over. Amid the din, with my face inches from the book, I pretended Daniel was still alive, sitting just across the table. If I looked up, I would see him.

I didn't look up. I didn't break the spell. I waited until the cafeteria had completely emptied before I went back to my room for the evening, so that I could imagine that Daniel, too, had departed with the crowd.

In my room now, I swallowed. My throat felt tight as a fist, but I'd cried enough. I watched the clock. At a few minutes before one a.m. I reached into my nightstand for Mr Monkey, just as if I had made a decision to do so. I took off his head and pulled out the little bag of weed. I held it. I hesitated only a few seconds.

Afterwards I slept as well as any corpse.

At breakfast the next morning I found myself trying to guess how much it would cost to buy a small amount of marijuana. I could scrape some money together. Maybe James gave new-customer discounts? Then I caught myself. I'd finish up Daniel's stash, possibly, but I wasn't going to buy any more. Even if it had helped me to sleep.

Sipping at my second glass of water, I found myself wondering again exactly how Daniel had financed his habit. When I'd thought he only smoked a little marijuana from time to time, I'd assumed he'd scavenged it from wealthier friends.

Worth Prentiss was known for his hospitality, as was Amanda Coates. But since it turned out Daniel had had a major problem, then how...

A male voice spoke. "Frances. OK to sit here?"

James, I thought uncontrollably, even though it wasn't his voice. I looked up, furious at myself, and then felt my eyes widen. It was George de Witt, Unity Vice President, friend of Saskia. Waiting with his tray, looking tentative.

It would have been far less surprising to find James there.

"Uh, sure," I said.

George plunked himself down across from me.

I resisted looking round the busy cafeteria. I didn't need to. I knew perfectly well there were half a dozen friends of George's sitting at a table by the large picture windows.

What was George de Witt doing here? I didn't know him very well, and before this second, I'd thought about him hardly at all. And he'd never paid any attention to me either. Though, I remembered, he had spoken up – however tentatively – against Patrick Leyden's plan at the Unity meeting.

Meanwhile, keeping his head down, George had begun to consume a very large breakfast. Toast. A heap of eggs. Sausages. Cereal. Two glasses of orange juice, one of milk. He didn't talk, or so much as glance at me; he ate. The scent of the sausages drifted across to me and made me feel a little queasy.

I drank more water.

Finally, after scraping his plate very nearly clean, George looked up. "How you doing?" he said.

"Fine."

George pushed himself up from the table. "Want anything?"

"Uh, no."

I watched in bemusement as George loped off towards the kitchen and then returned bearing another full plate and glass of milk. Feeling my eyes, he hunched a little defensively back into his seat and said, "I'm growing, OK?"

That, at least, was incontestable. At six foot four, George was the tallest boy in the school, and though he was probably not the thinnest, his height made him look it. The weird thing was that George had been in my maths class last year, and he'd been kind of tubby and short then.

Well, that was one possibility for fascinating conversation. "How much have you grown in the last year, George?" I asked.

He didn't look up. "Ten inches."

I couldn't think of anything else to say except "Oh," so I said nothing.

George drained the rest of his milk. He slammed his empty glass down on his tray. Then he looked up and across the table, straight into my eyes. He frowned.

We wouldn't have you even if you begged to join.

Being involved with Unity, doing good things, could do you a lot of good. I can talk to some of the kids – smooth things a little for you.

I discovered that I was holding my breath. I'd seen George and Saskia in intense conversation last night. Had Ms Wiles already spoken to them? Were they going to invite me? Did I want that?

"Frances?" George said.

"Yes?"

"You're OK, you know? Just how you are. You don't need to, you know, do anything. Or change. Or anything. You're fine. Like, how you are."

I stared at him. He was looking down now, not at me.

"Uh," I said. "Thanks. I think. Except I'm not sure exactly what you mean—"

George interrupted me. "I just wanted to say that you don't need to join Unity to be, you know, a good person." He stood up, hoisted his tray a little clumsily, said "Bye," and left, his legs covering ground even more rapidly than when he'd gone to the kitchen for seconds.

Only after an entire minute had passed was I aware that my jaw was gaping open. I closed it.

What on God's green earth had *that* been about? First James, and now George de Witt. Was Pettengill entirely populated by enigmatic boys? Or was this just another way of telling me I wasn't welcome?

I had the nagging feeling that somehow I'd stepped through Alice's looking glass. That things were happening beyond the rim of my ability to see or comprehend.

I couldn't deal. I just couldn't. I leaned my elbows on the table, rested my forehead on the backs of my hands, and longed passionately for... something. My mother might long for Nirvana; I'd settle for Oblivion.

Or... just someone to talk to. Somebody who made sense. Daniel, I thought automatically, and then rejected it, because I hadn't understood him either – or he me. I needed – I needed... James. No.

I sighed. I would go talk to Ms Wiles again. Maybe she was right.

In fact, I knew she was right. I would talk to her later today. I would tell her to do what she could. To talk to Patrick Leyden, or Saskia, or whoever. Smooth things over.

I would try joining Unity. I would participate. If Ms Wiles was right: if they'd have me.

14

Two days later, stomach churning, I sat in my room and watched the clock as it crept towards four thirty, when Saskia would be coming in one of the Unity Service vans to pick me up.

Things had happened fast. I could hardly believe it.

"We'll begin by giving you a tour of the food pantry," Saskia had said to me. From her polite face and demeanour, no one would have guessed that I'd insulted her and she'd shoved me at our last encounter. That she'd told me I wasn't welcome. "The tour will give you an idea of the scope of Unity's operations. I think you'll be impressed. Everyone always is."

"Thanks," I'd said feebly. I'd licked my lips, wondering how to venture an apology. Wondering how she and I would survive the alone-time together if I didn't.

It wasn't that she wouldn't meet my eyes. But there was nothing there when she did.

I hadn't apologised. Not yet. Today, though, I would.

I tried to untense my shoulders. On impulse I took Mr Monkey out of my bedside drawer and pulled off his head to check the bag. There wasn't very much marijuana left. I felt my mouth twist as I imagined how Daniel would laugh at me if he could see this. Oh, well. He'd be entitled.

I held the bag. The question was: did I most need to relax now, or would I need it more later on, after the tour, after I'd apologised to Saskia? The obvious answer was to wait, but I felt I needed to calm down now... and I was out of my mind! I stuffed the plastic bag back and impatiently threw Mr Monkey into my nightstand drawer again. I'd take a book and wait for Saskia downstairs, that was the best thing to do. I picked up my coat and my uncracked copy of *Beloved*, assigned for English, and headed out.

As I watched for the van, I reflected more calmly that it was just as well there was only enough weed left for two or three small cigarettes. Even though people claimed marijuana wasn't physically addictive, I already liked it too much and that would eventually pose a danger to me. I'd just finish up and then stop, that's all. I wasn't Daniel.

One thing, though. Maybe it was morbid, or perverse, or crazy, or all three. But I wished that once, just once, Daniel and I had got high together.

"When the weather's nice," Saskia said in a voice of determined chirpiness, "you can walk to the food pantry from school. It's in the old Harriman factory. Do you know it?"

I nodded. Harriman Leather Goods wasn't located far from Leventhal Shoes. "Don't your folks live close to there?" I asked Saskia, even though I knew the answer. I hated her little pretence of being a rich preppie. I wanted to make her say where she came from.

She hesitated for a fraction of a second. Then: "Yes. A block north. Behind Bettina's Convenience."

"Oh, that's right," I said, my voice rivalling hers for good cheer. "I remember now. Our school bus used to stop for you just outside the store."

Another pause, and then, surprisingly, Saskia seemed to loosen up. She glanced directly at me. "Those were the days," she said. "Middle-school busing. Ugh. You have to be glad *that* ended, right?"

I thought it was a rhetorical question, but when I didn't reply, Saskia repeated: "Right?"

"Uh-huh," I answered.

We were silent. I found myself dwelling obsessively, again, on how easily Saskia had slipped into life at Pettengill. It wasn't just her confidence and her beauty, she had all the little things too. Like clothes. Somehow, almost from freshman year on, she'd managed to dress well. Right now, for instance, she was wearing a nice red wool coat with a black velvet collar and leather gloves, and she had her hair pulled back off her forehead with a matching black velvet headband. And, again, the high-quality fake diamond earrings.

Daniel laughed in my head. *Besotted hankering after trinkets drags one down!*

I supposed Saskia might have a summer job. Something especially lucrative, obtained through her Unity contacts. Maybe she even worked for Patrick Leyden at his company. Although, wouldn't Daniel have said? Maybe not. Obviously, he hadn't told me everything – or much at all.

We drove through Lattimore's barren industrial district. I couldn't stop myself from staring at the boarded-up windows of Leventhal Shoes as we went past.

Unexpectedly Saskia said, "I hate this part of town. It reminds me of death. Whenever I'm here, I get a massive headache." She didn't move her eyes from the road.

She was talking about her own home. Still, after a second I said, "I know what you mean."

She pulled into the parking lot of the Harriman factory, then cut the van engine and faced me. Her lips were set in a hard line. "But that's just how it is, isn't it, Frances?" she said. "You have to deal with it. Work with it. Do what you have to do." She unbuckled her seat belt and got out of the van. So did I, with that feeling again of not understanding something.

Saskia was walking rapidly across the parking lot towards the door. I followed her.

A small yellow sign, obviously made on a laser printer and then laminated, had been affixed beside the back door of the building. It said UNITY FOOD PANTRY: PRIVATE. Apart from the sign, however, there was no clue that this was anything but an old abandoned factory. I felt the beginnings of the headache Saskia had just mentioned. I scurried up beside her and waited while she rang the bell.

Andy Jankowski answered. We blinked at each other in surprise. Then I remembered: he'd told me he worked here sometimes. *Pretend work. They have me watch the door.*

"Hi, Andy," I mumbled. For a reason I didn't understand, shame washed over me and I found I couldn't look straight at him.

"Hi, Andy!" said Saskia cheerily. "You on door duty this afternoon? Come on in, Frances." We stood in a small entryway furnished with an old kitchen chair and a space heater.

Andy closed the door behind us. "Yes," he said. "I sit in this chair and when someone rings, I let them in. Then I carry boxes to the vans. And from the vans." He paused as if thinking, and then added pointedly: "It's boring."

Saskia laughed. "I bet! OK, we go through here, Frances." I followed her through another door, but as I did, I glanced over my shoulder. Andy was just settling himself again into the chair. "Boring," he repeated softly. "I could do something else. If there *were* something else." His eyes were on mine. I thought he looked sad.

I shrugged helplessly at him. He shrugged back.

15

"OK," said Saskia as we moved into a giant open room. I looked around with interest.

This space had clearly once been the factory floor. Although it had now been emptied of everything connected with its past life, you could still see marks on the wide-planked floorboards where heavy machinery had once stood.

I could easily imagine those machines because, unlike this place, Leventhal Shoes had not been so comprehensively stripped. One rainy afternoon, the summer after we'd moved to Lattimore, Daniel had broken a window and we'd sneaked in to gawk at the grimy, useless old machines. For an instant the scene was vivid in my memory. If I were to close my eyes, I could almost be with Daniel again on that day. The way the musty air smelled, the creaking of the planks beneath our feet...

I kept my eyes open.

Saskia was gesturing largely at the room. Her voice had slipped into a singsong that told me she'd given this talk countless times. "As you can see, Unity has grown into much more than a food pantry, though we still tend to call it that. In fact, there's so much we do nowadays, the only real question is where to begin talking about it."

I nodded and gazed round the room as she spoke.

The factory floor had been divided into lots of different sections, each labelled with a handmade poster board sign. I could see "Canned and Dried Goods", "Women's Clothing", "Scholarship Programme", "Toys", "Children's Clothing", "Shoes", "Agency Referrals", "Packing and Transportation", "Emergency Cash Assistance", and, more mundanely, directly to our left in an enclosed section, "Office". There weren't many people around, although I could see the backs of a couple working in the "Packing" area. And in the "Emergency Cash Assistance" area, I recognised George de Witt with a cellular telephone clamped to his ear. He was intently taking notes on a piece of paper.

"Frances, let's dump our coats in the office before I give you the tour," Saskia said. "The heat in this place is always either completely on or completely off and, as you can tell, today it seems to be on."

It was stifling, I realised. Slowly I unbuttoned my coat, conscious that I was wearing what I suddenly thought of as an "Andy outfit" – an old flannel shirt and jeans. And Daniel's salvaged grey scarf round my neck. Meanwhile Saskia had revealed a deep blue boucle sweater. Very cute.

Why was I noticing her clothes so much today? I didn't know. She was always well dressed. It was nothing new.

Maybe she scavenged from the "Women's Clothing" area.

I followed her into the office where, to my surprise, we found Patrick Leyden. Did he never work at his own company? He was on the phone and immediately said, "Can you hold?" then put down the receiver and nodded at Saskia and me. "Frances, hello. Yvette told me you were rethinking things. I take it Saskia is showing you around?"

Yvette. That would be Ms Wiles. I nodded. I hated that he called her by her first name.

"Good for you," said Patrick Leyden blandly. He turned back to his phone call.

"This way," said Saskia, and I trailed, like a duckling, after her.

"We'll start in the canned goods area," she said, "because that was where Unity Service really began, as a food distribution pantry. And now, well, there are sixty-three branches of Unity Service at private high schools all over the country. And growing. All in just seven and a half years.

"It's all due to Pat – Mr Leyden, of course. It wasn't enough that he was applying to Harvard, but he had time during his senior year at Pettengill to found Unity as well. And now he's a millionaire at twenty-four, with his own company. And he's here quite a bit, as you just saw. Doesn't it just blow you away."

A statement, not a question. Her voice was so chirpy now that I thought I might have to throw something at her. I nodded instead.

"Anyway. Canned goods." Saskia escorted me to several banks of industrial shelving, stacked high with cans of corn and soup and green beans and – I squinted – mandarin oranges, and who knew what else. I listened while she talked about needy families getting monthly boxes, delivered by student-driven vans. "That's everyone's first job here, sorting cans into boxes for delivery.

You'll do it too. Like starting out in the mailroom of a company, Mr Leyden says."

I couldn't help myself. I said, "I suppose Daniel sorted cans here too, then?"

There was a short silence. Saskia reached up and wrapped a strand of hair round her finger. Finally she said, "Yes. We worked here together freshman year."

"Of course." I fixed my eyes on the stacks of cans again.

We moved on to some of the other areas. The clothing and toy areas were similar to canned goods; packages were made and goods went out, as needed. "Pretty basic," said Saskia. She was speaking more rapidly now, again as if she'd memorised lines. "We act as a central clearing house for donations and redistribution. Of course, these days we're pushing people to donate plain cash. That way we can buy what's most needed, and not be stuck redistributing useless stuff that people really ought to throw out. And the cash infusions have helped us open up the Emergency Cash Assistance and Scholarship Programmes, which are the most exciting things we're doing."

She didn't sound very excited.

"That's where the glamour is," said Patrick Leyden behind us. I jumped, hearing his voice. Saskia, however, had already turned round, smoothly. I did too. "That's where Unity's future is," he went on. "But of course I don't need to remind you two of that. Without the Scholarship Programme, neither of you would be here at all."

I couldn't help looking at Saskia. Was she angry to be lumped in with me? To be reminded of the scholarship?

She didn't seem to be. "Absolutely," she agreed.

Patrick Leyden looked at me straight on. "That's why I'm glad you've changed your mind, Frances. It shows something good about your character. And if, as Yvette said, you might be willing after all to help out with the Daniel Leventhal Memorial Fund Drive, I truly think you'd be a big help. We'd like to expand forcefully into the middle schools, and the story of your brother presents a unique opportunity for publicity."

I stood there.

Saskia was still smiling perkily.

"You don't have to decide right away," Patrick Leyden said to me. "I understand that you aren't sure yet. But Yvette said that you were willing to give it some time, and trust."

I thought uncontrollably of Andy's advice. *You can get up and go, Frances Leventhal. Nobody stops you.*

But I wouldn't leave. I had promised Ms Wiles. She understood things better than I did. I would hold on. I would participate.

Saskia was looking at me. So was Patrick Leyden. I groped and said, "I'm really impressed with the, um, food pantry. With everything here."

"Most people are impressed," said Patrick Leyden calmly. "And the more they learn, the more impressed they get."

I had heard James when he'd said not to create opportunities for violence. I believed in my gut that he knew, for whatever mysterious reason – a violent father? Some nasty situation at a previous school? A tough neighbourhood? – exactly what he was talking about.

Nonetheless, for a moment there, my palm seemed to throb with need, and I'd have given anything to smack Patrick Leyden.

16

I skipped dinner. I wasn't hungry. Back in my room I kicked off my boots and curled up on the bed to breathe in the lavender scent of the pillows. Usually just being in my room, alone and quiet, would calm me, and after a while my pulse did slow. But not completely, not to a normal rate. In fact, my whole body felt preternaturally tense, aware. I couldn't keep my eyes still; in tempo with my thoughts they flickered from one object in the room to another. What had I started? Could I really work for Unity? That project, using Daniel as a figurehead – using me as a figurehead – the thought of it still made me feel ill. And that environment, at the pantry, with dapper Patrick Leyden strutting around like a barnyard rooster in his gorgeous wool suits, Saskia jumping to attention every time he spoke: Yessir! Nosir! I supposed Daniel had jumped when Leyden spoke too: Everyone did. And I'd have to watch that all the time. I might even have to do it.

I took a deep breath then, because the fact was, I wasn't being reasonable and I knew it. The Unity food pantry was impressive. They helped hundreds of people with all kinds of serious, everyday, wrenching problems. Problems of poverty, of despair. Was I heartless to look at all that and not leap to help? Was I heartless still, even after Daniel's death? I had expected more from myself.

Patrick Leyden was actively doing something to help others. Who was I to question his methods? What had I ever done in my life? What did I want to do? Make art?

Art doesn't help anyone, Daniel had said.

I curled into a tight ball on the bed. If it weren't for Bubbe, who knows what would have happened to my own family after Sayoko left. Would my father have got some kind of job? Was he capable of that? It could be that the Leventhals had been, or at some point would be, only a breath away from needing services like the Unity food pantry. We had certainly needed the scholarships.

I sat up on the bed and leaned my back against the wall. OK, the expansion of the scholarship programme was a good cause. A *great* cause. There was no denying it. Patrick Leyden had talked on about it, his eyes fixed on mine. The dangerous environment in most urban public schools – even suburban schools – nowadays. Guns, violence, crowded classrooms, underpaid teachers, old books, and on and on.

"Maybe it will get fixed, Frances. Maybe the state and federal governments will move to save public education. Who knows? But it will take years, and every child we can help in the meantime – well, that's a child we can help."

Next to me, the telephone shrilled. I jumped. I never got phone calls; I conducted whatever small interpersonal business I had in person or via email. The phone rang again while I stared at it, and then I picked it up as if it were a grenade. "Hello?"

"Frances?" It was Ms Wiles. "I was just wondering how it went this afternoon."

Relief filled me at hearing her voice. "OK. Fine. I, um, I got a tour of the pantry. They do a lot of stuff there."

"Yes, they do."

"You've been there, haven't you, Ms Wiles?"

"Well, yes. Sometimes I pack boxes of food or clothes on Saturdays. I became interested right after I started here."

I was suddenly curious. "How many faculty members are actively involved with Unity?"

"Um, five or six, maybe." There was a pause, during which Ms Wiles seemed to be counting in her head. "Yes, five. Oh, and Andy Jankowski. Not that he's faculty. Or a volunteer."

The number surprised me. "I thought it was bigger. From stuff Daniel said, I guess."

"Well, people are busy. They come and go. I was only talking about the steady ones. Anyway, there's a big impact for the small number of people involved, relatively speaking. And you know, there are only about a dozen students who are truly involved. With maybe another couple of dozen on the periphery."

"Oh," I said. "Yes. I see."

There was a pause. Then: "Frances?" Ms Wiles's voice was heavy. "Listen, I can tell by your voice. You're not going to do this, are you? It's OK. It was just an idea, all right? If it doesn't work for you, it doesn't work for you."

"Well, I—"

"People are different. I'm disappointed, of course. But I understand."

I interrupted, hating the resignation in her voice. "Ms Wiles, stop! I didn't say I wasn't going to do it!"

Another pause. "Your voice said it for you, Frances. It's fine, really. I just wanted to help you."

"Ms Wiles, it's just..."

"What?"

I blurted it out. Well, part of it: I couldn't talk about Saskia. I said, "I can't stand Patrick Leyden!"

There was a moment of incredulous silence, and then Ms Wiles began to laugh. And then to roar.

"Ms Wiles?"

"Oh, God, Frances – who *can*?"

"What?" I couldn't believe it. "You don't like him? but I thought you said..."

Ms Wiles calmed down finally. "Frances, sweetheart, I love you, but you're so naïve. No one with any sensibility at all – and you have lots – could possibly like Patrick Leyden. On the personal level, he's a complete dickhead." I heard her chuckle again.

Dickhead. I was stunned. "I don't understand. Everybody loves him—"

"No. Everyone *pretends* to love him," Ms Wiles said. "OK, who knows, maybe some people really do. I sure don't, though."

"But everyone acts like he's God." And Daniel had truly thought so, I added silently. I couldn't have been mistaken about that. Daniel had adored and admired Patrick Leyden. Although I wondered if Saskia honestly did too...

Ms Wiles was replying thoughtfully. "Well, there are different rules for the rich and successful, that's all. Behaviour gets tolerated, even lauded, in rich people that wouldn't be in ordinary people. Maybe some even fool themselves. They kiss ass but tell themselves that's not really what they're doing." She laughed again, a quick gurgle. "I have to admit, it can be amusing to watch."

My bewilderment was beginning to change into some kind of relief. If Ms Wiles agreed with me about Patrick Leyden, then all was well. I was still a bit confused, though. "But you recommended I work with him. With Unity."

"Yes." Her voice was suddenly serious and firm. "And I still do."

"But if he's such a—" I discovered that I couldn't say *dickhead* to my teacher, even though she had used it herself a moment ago. "—such a jerk, then I don't understand."

"The best leadership doesn't always come from the people you'd pick as your friends, Frances. Sometimes you have to be able to work with – and for – someone you dislike, for the purpose of a higher goal."

"Oh," I said, then we both fell silent.

When Ms Wiles spoke again, her voice was very gentle. "But more importantly, Frances, I think you need to participate in something. Even if you have to force yourself a little bit. You need to be part of something that involves other people. It will do you good."

"Oh," I said again, cringing. Beneath her words, I heard all kinds of things that she hadn't actually said. Did *she* see me as a pathetic loner too, then? I supposed she must.

Another long silence.

"Well," said Ms Wiles finally. "I need to go now, Frances. But think a little more about what I've said, OK?"

I couldn't bear to have her think me pathetic. I needed – needed—

If it ought to be done, then apply yourself to it strenuously, Daniel said in my head. I could almost see him, looking down at his folded hands and with that supercilious Buddha-quoting expression on his face.

"Wait," I said. "I've thought enough. I know you're right. I'll join Unity and help out all I can. I've made up my mind."

And I felt a great peace sweep over me. This, at long last, was the right decision.

17

I was looking at *Beloved*, which I still hadn't even begun reading, when the phone rang again. Twice in one evening? Maybe it was Ms Wiles calling back. I answered tentatively.

The voice was feminine, sweet, assured – and somehow also tense. "Frances? I'm in your dorm right now. Downstairs. I want to talk to you. Can I come up?"

She hadn't identified herself, but then, she didn't need to. It was Saskia.

I reminded myself that I was going to join Unity and that, as Ms Wiles had said, I'd need to work with people I maybe didn't like.

"Yes," I said. I cleared my throat and said it again more strongly. "Yes, sure." And then, hating myself but feeling it was best to start on a friendly note, added sweetly: "Please come up."

"See you in a second, then," said Saskia.

Numb, I put down the phone. Frantically my eyes scanned the room and my heart rate increased again. My place, mine – private! I was stupid and slow. Why hadn't I just said I'd come down?

Then I heard an imperious triple rap at the door. It was too late for second thoughts. I tried to relax. I moved to let Saskia in.

In my room the jarring effect (which I love) is caused by the way the "normal" things – the quilt, the pillows, the rag rugs – clash with the ferocity and darkness of the acrylic paintings on the walls.

My paintings.

There are three of them. One is relatively large, the others smaller. I can't describe them well, except to say that I'm still not the Picasso fan that Ms Wiles is. I have no desire to emulate him in any way. It's not that I don't agree he was a genius. It's that – well, he was a little too deliberate, a little too controlled, for my taste. He always knew what he was doing.

Me, I like it when artists just throw things into their paintings. I like a sense of danger and risk; a *lack* of control. It's hard to explain, especially since achieving that particular effect in a piece of art actually requires a tremendous amount of control. Of your medium. Of your hands. Of yourself. You create, very precisely, something that is – wild.

At least, that's how it is for me.

Not that I think my paintings fully achieved that wildness. I'm not good enough yet, that's the simple truth. But there's definitely something there, on those canvases. Ms Wiles said it best.

Nightmares.

The blank squares – dark green, dark blue, black mixed with yellow – that you see when you first look at the paintings are not what you see when you keep looking. They're only what I painted on top, at the end. It's a very thin coat, as thin as I could manage, as thin as would cover and conceal, while not concealing.

Beneath that coat of paint are all my secret emotions, expressed fully and frankly. You can't see them at all in the finished paintings – except you can. You can *feel* them. You look at my paintings, and you know they're there. Beneath the dark squares.

They are mine, those paintings.

"Oh!" Saskia exclaimed. I saw with satisfaction that she took an involuntary step back, away from the biggest acrylic. She was quite silent after that, standing in the middle of my room, looking. Then she moved from one to another, slowly, and – it was a hideous, unwelcome surprise to me – her face illuminated with genuine pleasure. I looked at her, and I saw how wonderfully her dark tresses framed her face, and how her beauty contrasted with the darkness of what I'd painted... and I felt like some creature out of the swamps.

How could she possibly like my work? It wasn't meant to be liked! Only *I* could like it.

"I had no idea," said Saskia finally, swinging round. "Just no idea at all. I mean, Daniel said you were an artist and everything, but I never saw – my God. I'm so impressed. These are so good. They give me the *creeps*." She moved closer to the smallest painting, the murky greenish one. "Wow." She put out her hand.

"Hey!" I said sharply. "Don't touch!"

She snatched her hand back. "Sorry." She said it as if she meant it.

"Sorry," I said also, after a second. "I get a little possessive. And they're, well, fragile."

Saskia said, "I understand." She moved slightly more towards me, but she didn't come as confidently close as she had in the past. And she was still looking around carefully, as if she too had stepped through the looking glass into a world full of strange and surprising objects. As if she wasn't sure what to do or say next. She frowned.

I couldn't think of anything to say either. I stared at her stupidly. I watched her continue to scan the room and its contents: the pillows heaped on my bed, the rumpled quilt where I'd just been lying down, the carefully ironed white cotton curtain on the small single window, the dark corner next to it...

Where the mirror was. Screaming – once you noticed it – in its own way.

Saskia's eyes widened and she took a step towards it, her brow furrowing. "Frances, what's that?"

"It's a Jewish custom," I said tensely. "You drape the mirrors in black when you're in mourning. You're not supposed to look at yourself or think about yourself."

There was a moment of silence in which Saskia regarded me carefully. Then: "But only for a *week*," she said. "Only while you sit shivah. Right?" And yes, that was the familiar Saskia voice, the one I loved to hate, with its derisive undertone.

My own familiar response snapped into place too. "I'm still in mourning," I shot back.

Saskia lifted her chin. "So am I," she said. "I'm just a little less theatrical about it."

And, just like that, dislike shimmered naked in the air between us, on both sides. *The wise find peace on hearing the truth.* Now *there* was an aphorism that was absolutely correct. "What did you come here for, Saskia?" I asked bluntly.

Saskia smiled, and for once it wasn't a pretty sight. "To tell you that I haven't changed my mind. I don't want you involved with Unity. I want you to tell Patrick no, and then go back into your cave. Just go back to doing whatever it is that you do. Stomping around alone on campus. Draping mirrors in black. Painting." She waved towards the walls. "Whatever. Just stay out of Unity."

"Really," I said.

"Really," she mimicked. Her face was very hard. Her cheeks were suddenly flushed. "Come on, Frances. It's not like you have any great personal attraction to charity work. I'm not fooled. Neither are you. And – Daniel wouldn't be either."

That hurt, but I wouldn't show it. "Then why do you think I'm—"

Saskia cut right in. "Guilt, I suppose. Or you're tired of being such an outcast. Frankly, I don't care what your reasons are." She took a step closer to me, and then another.

I remembered her shoving me, and I backed up a bit.

"It's not my business to wonder why, after two and a half years, you suddenly think it's a good idea to work with Unity. It *is* my business" – Saskia's eyes narrowed – "to tell you that I just won't have it. I said it before, and it stands: *You are not welcome.*"

My own cheeks were flushed now too, I could feel their heat. I was afraid, I suddenly realised. I could feel it in my pounding pulse.

Another truth: I had always been afraid of Saskia.

I didn't want to show my fear. I managed to say, "Patrick Leyden wants me. So what do you think you can do about it?"

Saskia's voice was steady. "Quite a bit, actually. Wallace and George and – well, *everybody* is with me on this. So if you push yourself in, we'll make your life at school a living hell. I promise you, Frances. If you join Unity, then soon you'll really, really wish you hadn't."

I couldn't believe this was happening. I said stupidly, "I'll tell Patrick Leyden that you said all this and—"

Saskia shook her head. "And who do you think he'll believe? You or me? Who's established trust with him for years? He's seen your reluctance. He'll think you're making it all up to get out of working on the memorial project. He'll think you're a flake."

She stopped and just looked at me out of that icy face.

We'll make your life at school a living hell.

I was aware that, in a moment, I might start trembling. I hadn't quite acknowledged it, but I'd feared what Saskia was describing since I'd started at Pettengill. It was any outcast's nightmare.

If I looked carefully, I suspected I might find it beneath the black paint of the small acrylic by the window.

"Did you hear me, Frances?" said Saskia. "Did you understand me?" And when I still didn't reply, she added, "I'll spell it out, then. One more time.

"Keeping you out of Unity – that's *my* little memorial to Daniel. Upholding what he would have wanted. I'm going to do it, Frances. I promise you."

I looked into her beautiful frozen eyes and I believed every word she said. And I found myself nodding as if impelled – just as I'd nodded when James lectured me about violence.

"Quit," Saskia instructed. "Quit before you get started. Do it however you want. Letter to Patrick. Email. Phone call. I don't care. Just do it. Do you understand me?"

I nodded again.

"Say it," Saskia commanded.

"Yes," I said as if I were hypnotised.

"Good," said Saskia, like she was praising a dog. She showed me all her teeth. They weren't perfect, two were crooked. And then, between one breath and the next, she was gone.

Alone, I sat down on the edge of my bed. I held my elbows tightly and I felt my whole body shake.

I hated her. I hated her for reflecting my own weakness, my own fears, back at me. I hated her for seeming to see into my paintings so clearly, and then for pulling out a nightmare and hurling it straight at me. And it was clear now that *she* really hated *me* too. It was irrational that that would hurt so much.

Artists aren't rational, I guess.

I didn't know what to do. Go on as I always had, as Saskia wanted? Or take Ms Wiles's advice, try to become a better, more giving, more participatory person – and face Saskia's wrath? Both roads seemed impossible. Impassable. How had this happened? I had never wanted anything to do with Unity!

After a minute I reached out and groped, blindly, in the nightstand drawer for Mr Monkey and my pathetic inheritance from Daniel. I needed whatever comfort I could find.

18

The next day was Saturday. I had a couple of morning classes, but with a twinge of guilt I stayed in bed through most of the first one. I figured I could probably still take advantage of the depressed, in-mourning-for-brother loophole. Why not? It was true. It just wasn't the whole truth.

Getting high last night had not actually helped.

I did go to my second period class, an art open studio. This was free work time, and Ms Wiles was not supposed to be there. I was relieved, I didn't think I could face her today.

For nearly two hours I worked in silence on my elephant femur and it did soothe me a little, to work the clay with my hands. Some of the time I eavesdropped on two of the other girls in the studio, Theresa Quinn and Tonia Mack. I wondered distantly what was wrong with me, that I'd never made an effort to befriend even nice people like them. I knew that if I had friends, I would be less vulnerable to Saskia. But it was too late now. You couldn't approach people when you were desperate. They'd smell your neediness and fear. They'd reject you automatically.

Still, I listened wistfully as they chattered. SATs, a dream Tonia had had and what it might mean, Theresa's boyfriend's telephone call last night, an approaching history quiz, a favourite shirt of Tonia's that had suspiciously disappeared from the dryer. It was like they were in some other country, speaking another language. There was no way to bridge the gap.

It was weird to realise that always before I'd seen the gap as being about the fact that I was on a scholarship, or that I was shy, small, freakish-looking. Ten million reasons that suddenly seemed like half-truths. Was there something deeper in me that kept others at a distance?

The period ended. Tonia and Theresa and the others left. I slowly wrapped my sculpture in wet rags to preserve it until next time, and as I did so, dread descended fully upon me. I couldn't hide in bed or the art studio for ever. Right now, for instance, I had to go to lunch. Having skipped dinner last night and breakfast this morning, I was, despite myself, hungry.

I wondered bleakly if Daniel had felt anything like this – this senselessness, this fear, this despair – before he overdosed. I realised he must have despised me. Why else would Saskia be so sure he'd be pleased with her actions?

I had to lean against the wall for a minute or two. Then I put on my coat and marched myself over to the cafeteria and my fate.

Just after I arrived, I saw Andy Jankowski a few people ahead of me in the cafeteria line, carefully helping himself to a couple of grilled cheese sandwiches and a heap of tomato slices. He looked so innocent, so absorbed in his task. I was filled with a wash of warmth for him. I lifted a hand to wave, but he was turned half away and didn't see me. I let my hand drop. I thought about calling out, but I didn't want to draw attention to myself.

Andy, like all resident faculty and staff members, was entitled to eat as much school food as he wanted. But it was rare to actually encounter him in the cafeteria – although I did suddenly have a memory of seeing him talking with a woman who served food there, a quiet, nervous-seeming woman I hadn't seen in weeks. The other "mentally challenged" Pettengill employee. People had tended to greet her overloudly or not at all. That included me. I couldn't even remember her name. She had been nearly invisible... like Andy. Like me?

I wondered where that woman had gone. I wondered what it had been like for Andy, when he was a kid, when he went to school. It would have been twenty or more years ago, of course. Had he been in a regular school, or a special one? Had other kids tormented him? Had he been lonely? Had he welcomed invisibility, in the way that I – sort of – did?

Was Sayoko ever lonely in her monastery? My mother had chosen isolation – like me, I suddenly thought. Whereas my father had just accepted it, maybe. Unless that was also a choice?

Andy reached the end of the line. He transferred his food to a large lunchbox he'd brought, then walked quietly out of the cafeteria. The double doors swung easily shut behind him. The din continued. People moved up the line, banged trays, grabbed food, bugged the servers.

Invisible. Or a target. Were those the only possibilities for me?

I wasn't going to cry. Not here, not now. I was not. I was not, I was not—

"Hey, Frances!" I swivelled. James! His abrupt appearance startled me – thank God – right out of crying. My heart involuntarily sped up, but it was just that his was a friendly voice...

"There are people in line behind you," James continued, "so pick a dessert already." He deftly slid in ahead of two kids and into place behind me in line, grabbed two puddings, and dumped one on my tray. "Let's go!" He grinned down at me. "How ya doing?"

I couldn't help it. I smiled back up at him. "Hi," I said.

His sweatshirt said QUANTICO. It was dark blue, and I had to admit he looked good in that colour. His hair was loose, for once, on his shoulders. Brown waves, very soft.

"Haven't seen you lately," he said. "Where you been?" James looks at you when he talks to you. He watches your face – your eyes, your lips – like it matters to him what you say.

A small rubber ball had taken up residence in my chest and was bouncing wildly between my throat and my lungs. "Around," I managed to answer.

"So, you OK these days?"

"Yes," I said. "I'm fine."

"Yeah?" He was still looking at me. Looking right down into my eyes. *You.*

I wanted to take a deep breath, but I couldn't. There wasn't enough air in the cafeteria for anything but a shallow gulp.

Oh. My. God.

Ms Wiles had been right.

I was in love with a small-time prep school drug dealer.

19

We had reached the end of the cafeteria line. "You wanna find a table?" said my amoral love.

James was willing to eat lunch with me? And, presumably, to talk to me? I required nothing more. "Sure," I said dizzily.

"Any preference where?"

"No." I was reduced to words of one syllable. It was all I could do to speak. I followed James, eyes on his shining fall of hair, on his strong shoulders, on his hips in their faded jeans as he threaded his way through tables. All my other problems suddenly seemed like so much accumulated dust. While this one... or maybe it wasn't a problem?

I didn't *feel* like it was a problem. I felt wonderful! Spring was in the air! Flowers blossomed where I stepped! And at any moment the soundtrack would swell. I couldn't help wondering what music would be most appropriate. Something classic? Bonnie Raitt? Edith Piaf? No, it should be strange and new and lovely. It occurred to me that love was the root of the word lovely, and this seemed a miraculous discovery, a fact of immense significance.

I was going to read that book *Beloved*. Soon. Today.

But even as I had these thoughts, I knew I was nuts. I knew it was unlikely that James would love me back. I wasn't pretty, or sexy, or witty, or popular, or anything desirable. And drug dealer or not, he was far above my social station. I didn't have a station at all, come to think of it. But... I hadn't heard that he was going out with anyone, not once since he'd started school here in the fall, in fact. That was something. Unless he was gay, which he couldn't be, not the way he looked at girls. Even at me, just now.

And he was always nice to me. Always said hi, how are you. He'd defended me at the Unity meeting. In fact, he'd been practically my knight in shining armour there – he'd taken on Patrick Leyden himself. Imagine that.

The full extent of James's extraordinary nature was now clear to me. Except for the drug dealing part. But everyone had faults.

And suppose by some miracle James did like me? Could I get him to abandon his evil ways? Of course, I would need to give up marijuana myself, or I wouldn't make a credible reformer. It was a good thing I hadn't had time to get to like it too much. I resolved to flush the remaining weed down the toilet just as soon as I got back to my dorm.

Ahead of me James had found a table that had two empty seats facing each other at one end. He put his tray down and pushed it across the table, moving round the edge to sit across from the empty seat that was for me. Happily I put my own tray down and sat. We would talk. I would try, delicately, to get a sense of whether he felt anything for me...

"Hey," James said easily to the table at large.

I looked to my right. Only then did the faces at the table resolve themselves from blurs into actual people. Unity people. We were sitting at the table where Unity members sat. I was, myself, right next to George de Witt.

It was like being hit in the face by a bucketful of cold water. No. Acid. Something that burned everything else away.

Automatically I scanned the rest of the table. It could have been worse; Saskia was at the other end, well away from me. Nonetheless, she was looking over. I forced myself to meet her gaze. It was empty, icy, like yesterday. After a second she turned her shoulder and continued her conversation.

I looked across at James. His mouth was full. He nodded at me genially, cluelessly, and then chased down his mouthful with half a glass of chocolate milk. "Cold out there today, huh?" he said. "Just getting across the quad, I thought my butt would freeze off."

Small talk, James style. It was no colder today than it had been the day before, or the day before that. "Yeah," I said. I looked down at my plate. Stuffed shells with tomato sauce. Carrots. A roll and butter. The chocolate pudding James had got for me.

I had been hungry not long ago.

I stabbed a carrot with my fork and put it in my mouth. I chewed. I swallowed. I looked again at James. He was still beautiful, even with a milk moustache. I imagined myself sitting on his lap and licking it off. I thought about Daniel's cache of condoms.

No! I wasn't in love with James! I wasn't stupid and I wasn't self-destructive. I was infatuated, maybe. But James was a goddamned drug dealer and, worse, he had brought me here to sit amongst my enemies.

Rage filled me. I was a fool to have forgotten even for a few minutes who I was, and what was going on in my world, and that I had a decision I needed to make. A decision that felt as if it were – though I knew it couldn't really be – mortal.

Suddenly, between one carrot and the next, I had decided. I'd die before I'd let Saskia Sweeney think she had intimidated me. I'd die before I'd disappoint Ms Wiles. And, finally, I wouldn't be a wimp in front of James. Even if he had no clue what was going on. I wouldn't be – what was it he'd called me at that Unity meeting? – a kicked kitten.

"Saskia?" I called out down the table. Did I imagine it, or did most of the kids sitting there turn to look at me? "Saskia," I repeated, "I wanted to ask you – I need to sign up for my first shift at the food pantry. Stacking cans or doing whatever. Tomorrow afternoon would work for me. Is that OK?"

Saskia stared at me. Her lips pursed.

"Hey, could you do the noon to two o'clock shift?" Pammy Rosenfeld asked. She was sitting halfway down the table. "We need someone else there. I think a shipment of Green Giant corn and peas came in yesterday." She smiled at me. "I'm in charge of scheduling this month."

Clearly Pammy was not in on Saskia's little plan. Maybe Saskia had been exaggerating? Speaking only for herself?

"OK," I said directly to Pammy. "I'm in."

"Thanks," said Pammy. "Welcome."

"Thank you," I said calmly. I did not look at Saskia. I looked across at James, trying to think of something innocuous to say. He was frowning as if puzzled—

"Oops!" said George de Witt, beside me. Only then – I swear it was after he spoke – did he elbow his second, full plate right off his tray.

The tomato sauce-soaked contents slid right into my lap. Startled, I yelped and looked at George – and he looked back, his eyes empty. Icy.

Saskia had not been bluffing. If I went ahead with this, so would she. She would make my life miserable.

Maybe I went a little bit crazy then. Or maybe I was still under the influence of the defiance that had just impelled me to challenge Saskia. I recall having the vague thought that I was *already* miserable; could it really get any worse?

I found myself shouting, "Food fight!" I grabbed my plate and ejected its contents directly into George's face.

"Hey!" George yelled as I flung the dish away to the left. I heard it smash as it hit the floor, or a table, or the wall, or wherever. It sounded like a thunderclap.

I watched as a stuffed shell slid off George's nose, fell to his chest, and then softly plopped down on to his jeans, leaving a blood-like trail of tomato sauce in its wake. It all seemed to happen in slow motion.

Around me – I could sense it even in the midst of my little fit – the entire cafeteria had come to a complete staring halt.

George's expression was profoundly satisfying.

At that point I began giggling, and found I couldn't stop. I had no control over myself. I roared. I wailed. I descended into convulsions of hysteria and had to clutch my stomach. Inside, I panicked. I wondered if you could die of laughter. Maybe it wasn't a bad way to go, but this was hurting...

"Get a teacher!" I heard vaguely. "Run, quick!"

Then I felt somebody grab me by the shoulders and slap me, hard, across the right cheek. And then the left. Vaguely, I was relieved. I hiccuped for a minute or two, eyes closed, aware of the horror and shock and titillation of everyone around me. Then I opened my eyes and saw that, of course, it was James before me, one hand on my shoulder, his right hand still upraised.

"Creating an opportunity for violence?" I said. I was surprised; the words came out calmly, even quietly. I held his eyes. I was aware that my own were filled with tears. Several had dripped down my face. "Or was that just payback?"

James's voice was even quieter. I doubted that anyone but me could hear it. "No, Frances." And then, as two teachers came running up, I saw his lips move. No sound came out, and I hadn't realised I had lip-reading skills, but somehow I thought he was saying: "Oh, God. I don't know what to do."

20

I was given a bed in the school infirmary for the night. Mention was made of a regular group therapy session in managing grief, held on Wednesday evenings at Lattimore Hospital. Ms Wiles telephoned me, and so did my father. I told everyone I was very tired. I told everyone I was sorry. I told everyone that yes, I had been trying to suppress my despair over Daniel's death, but that I could no longer manage alone and some help would be very welcome. If I had support, I said, then yes, I thought I could continue with school. I said again that I was very sorry. That I didn't want to be a trouble to anyone.

There, there, people said. Everyone assured me that I'd get all the help and support I needed. Individual counselling too, if that was deemed appropriate, said the school nurse.

It felt as if there were someone else in my body, propped up in the infirmary bed, listening, nodding, saying what people wanted to hear. It was nice. I felt calm.

In the background, I was thinking. I was thinking oddly well.

When I was finally alone, I picked up the telephone with a steady hand. I dialled Saskia's room. She answered on the first ring. And although I had not consciously planned a speech, I found that I knew exactly what to say, and that I was not in the least afraid.

"It's Frances. Listen, if you or your friends do anything to me ever again, I *promise*, I'll keep on reacting like a crazy person. It will freak everyone out. Like George today. I saw his eyes. He thought he'd pushed me over the edge and it terrified him. He's a nice guy, strangely enough. He won't lift a finger against me ever again. We both know that, Saskia.

"And maybe I really am just an inch away from insanity. I might be. I don't know. Do you want to be the one who shoves me there? Do you want that on your tiny conscience? Even if *you* don't mind, your so-called friends will. Like George. You might find you don't have as many allies as you thought."

I hung up without waiting for her reply.

I knew I could join Unity now if I wanted. I could do as I pleased there, and Saskia would do nothing about it. At the very least I had a period of reprieve. Breathing space.

But I didn't have any sense of victory.

A little later they served me dinner on a tray, and then gave me a pill. I fell into a deep, artificial sleep.

It was as if I were in a kind of trance, rather than a dream. I was aware of myself, of my body, prone on my back beneath a cotton blanket in the infirmary bed. I was aware of the lids of my eyes, heavy, leaden.

Then I was elsewhere. It was cold, above my head were stars. And I was climbing, climbing the steep snowy side of a mountain. I was wearing some kind of robe, my feet and hands were bare, and even in the dark, and beset by the fierce winter wind, I seemed to know exactly how to move up the rock face. Doggedly I kept finding toe and fingerholds. And there was nothing but the present moment, nothing but the grim climb and something inside me, impelling me upward.

Then I was at the top of the mountain, scrambling to my feet, panting.

Before me was the entrance to a cave. And no sooner did I see it than, without moving, I was within it. Within it, and on my knees.

There, legs crossed in the lotus position, sat Daniel. His face was mocking as ever, but his voice was serene. *You know the rules, Frances. You may ask one question. If I answer, you will die.*

I said: *I understand.*

Daniel smiled. The smile was not kind.

Terror gripped me, but my mouth opened, and I blurted: *Daniel, I have to know. Did you really kill yourself?*

The words and the thought were liberated. Speaking had made the question real. It hung suspended like an icicle.

As I watched, Daniel shook his head slowly from side to side.

Daniel! I said. *Daniel, brother—*

But suddenly I was falling through space at a furious speed. My last thought was that screaming would be useless – and that I had made a terrible, terrible mistake.

21

On Sunday morning after breakfast I was permitted to leave the infirmary, and I went to the Unity food pantry for my first shift, exactly as I'd told Pammy Rosenfeld I would. I trudged over from Pettengill, and was surprised to feel my mood improve a little bit with the exercise and the clear sky.

Then I passed the old Leventhal shoe factory, and felt myself tighten.

I didn't want to think about my dream, or nightmare, but I did. I had woken remembering it very clearly, and feeling disturbed. But surely it meant nothing; dreams were the garbage dumps of the mind. And it wasn't so hard to discard a nightmare. Not when you were walking outside on a sunny, mild winter's day. Not if you concentrated.

I wondered why it was that I hadn't had a sexy dream about James instead. Just my luck.

Determinedly I filled my lungs with fresh air. I would simply follow Ms Wiles's advice, I decided, and participate in life. I wouldn't think too much. I would put the stuff I didn't care to deal with behind me. I would work on my art, and maybe I would see if I could befriend Tonia Mack and Theresa Quinn. All I had to do to start was smile and say hi. And the grief therapy group – I did like the sound of that. Other people would talk, and I could listen. Or I could tell them my dream and they'd all say they'd had similar experiences, similar delusions, and I'd be comforted.

But I got to the food pantry and realised that I didn't believe a word of it.

Andy Jankowski opened the door for me, however, and that did make me feel better. I was surprised at the gladness I felt. "Andy! Good morning!"

He blinked a little at my smile, but then, pleased, he gave me a big one in return. "Hello, Frances Leventhal."

I dropped my voice. "How's the pretend work going? Are you still bored out of your mind?"

"I'm used to it." Andy looked at me with interest. "Are you here to do pretend work too, Frances Leventhal?"

"I think they're going to have me unpack cans of vegetables," I said, wondering again why the Unity people didn't find Andy perfectly competent to do that also. "Or something like that."

Andy nodded. "Pretend work, yes. All fake work."

I blinked. "No, there's cans and things to stack. Packing. I don't know why they don't let you—"

Andy scowled. Abruptly he opened the inner door and began walking towards the office area, where I could see Pammy, sitting alone at a desk. I scurried after him. "In there," Andy said.

I had hurt his feelings. I watched his back as he retreated to his post. Then I looked over at Pammy, who was staring at me with her mouth open. "Hey," I said shyly.

"Hey," said Pammy. "Um. Frances. I wasn't – that is, I didn't think you'd come today."

"But I said I would." After a second I swallowed and added, "I'm fine, Pammy. Really. Truly." I looked her in the eyes. "I want nothing more than to help out here."

"Oh. Good." Pammy bit her lip. "That's good." She looked down nervously at some papers in front of her. "The thing is, I didn't bother to – I don't have anyone scheduled to work with you after all." A pause. "I suppose I could call someone. Or people will be coming in, and maybe someone could... your shift doesn't start until noon." She trailed off, frowning deeply.

"Well, whatever," I said. "But it's just sorting and stacking cans, right? I'm sure I could handle it if you just showed me what you needed." *Even if I did flip out yesterday,* I thought bitterly. Then I admonished myself. I was going to be friendly and cooperative.

"Well, we always have new people work in pairs. Let me look at the schedule again... you're early." I waited. "OK," Pammy said, after studying a paper for a minute. "OK, it's fine. Wallace is supposed to come – he'll show you what to do. In the meantime, I can just explain the basics."

"Fine," I said. Wallace was a friend of Saskia's too. But – I straightened my shoulders – it would be good to test things right away. Find out if I really had thwarted Saskia. "Explain everything," I said to Pammy.

We walked over to the canned vegetable area, and I focused carefully on Pammy as she talked, finding it hard not to roll my eyes. It wasn't exactly rocket science. There were a bunch of battered cartons that contained canned vegetables of various kinds. The cans were to be sorted by vegetable and transferred to the metal utility shelves. No more than four cans were to be stacked on top of each other. I was to create no fancy pyramids or other structures, but simply perform basic stacking. "Corn here," Pammy said, pointing. "Peas there, carrots there, beets there."

"I get it," I said.

Pammy had one eye on the door. "I don't understand why nobody's here yet," she fretted. "Usually one or two people come early."

"I think I can start with the cans anyway."

She kept frowning. "You'll need the large stepladder. I'm not sure where it is. I want the corn up high, on that top shelf. I know the shelf below's empty, but the corn really belongs on the top."

"OK," I said. "Isn't that a stepladder right over there?"

She swivelled. "Yes. OK... Wallace should be along shortly."

"I can handle it," I said in my best good-girl voice. "You go back to the office, do whatever you need to do. I'll come find you if I have questions—" I saw her frown, so I swiftly switched gears. "Or you could check up on me every so often. Just until Wallace comes, of course."

"Yes, that's true," Pammy said. "I'll check and see how you're doing every few minutes. Until Wallace or someone else gets here." Her brow finally cleared. Mostly. She turned, and then swung back hesitantly. "Frances? I know I must seem overly anxious, but... well, you have to understand, everything is done here according to a system. If the cans aren't stacked right, with everything in its expected place, then it's much harder for a whole crew to work here and, well, you know, quickly pack up a variety box for a family."

"I can see that," I said, though a little voice in the back of my head was thinking sourly, *Andy's right, it's all fake work.* I smiled at her and went to get the stepladder, and finally she left as I put it into position.

The cardboard cartons were haphazardly thrown on the floor, their flaps already open. They looked like they'd been through a United Nations food drop. The cans inside each carton weren't even uniform in size. I shrugged, and began climbing the ladder and stacking cans. Climbing the ladder and stacking cans.

You're the only scholarship recipient in Unity's history who hasn't joined the organisation. Who hasn't helped out, who hasn't given back.

I wiped my dusty hands on my jeans. So this was giving back. Helping out. Participating.

After a while I felt less exasperated with Pammy, because it became clear that it *would* actually be much more efficient to do this work with a partner. One person below, handing up the cans, the second on the ladder, stacking. I was getting tired.

Andy was just sitting by the door, wanting something to do. And OK, maybe this work was pretty silly too, but... I headed back to the office.

As I approached, I could hear Pammy's voice, high and anxious, asking a question. And someone else's. Wallace.

The office door was ajar an inch or two. For some reason that I couldn't articulate – maybe because Pammy sounded so anxious? – I didn't knock or make my presence known. Instead I paused just outside and, astonished at myself but also somehow excited, shamelessly eavesdropped.

"I'm not sure that's what Patrick wants," Wallace was saying. His voice wasn't loud, but it was perfectly audible if I strained. Which, suddenly fearless, I did.

Wallace had gone on. "Saskia says he's really pissed off about the shipment mix-up and he feels that all the customers need to be reimbursed. Or given a replacement order for free. Their choice."

Customers? That was a weird word to use for the recipients of charity. Free replacement order? Wasn't everything free anyway?

"So he wants us to call all of them *personally* and ask which they want?" Pammy sounded incredulous.

"Well, all the alums, yeah. He says that's the professional thing to do. They *are* our partners, you know."

Alums? Partners? Customers? Were those words being used interchangeably?

Pammy wailed, "But that's several dozen calls! What about email? Can't we just—"

"No. And Saskia said to do what Patrick wants."

A silence. Then: "She always says that."

"Pammy."

"I know, I know." Pammy exhaled audibly. "But I have so much going on—"

Wallace's voice rose. "Do you think I *don't*? Be smart. This is our job. Our future depends on doing it well."

Behind the door, I realised that my heart was now pounding wildly. What were they talking about?

There is something wrong here, I thought. I knew it with the same certainty that occasionally came to me when I painted, when I knew I had a tight hold on something true – even if I wasn't sure exactly what it was.

I felt my feet backing up. I returned to the stepladder. I stacked and stacked, and eventually Wallace came and helped me, mostly in silence. His expression was closed, internal. He did nothing to make me personally anxious.

Fake work, whispered Andy's voice in my head. *Pretend work*.

22

I had dinner that night with my father at Bubbe's house. It was a tension-filled meal during which my father said little beyond: "You really are feeling better? Good, good." But he kept looking at me, his expression anxious, hopeless. He had opened a couple of cans of lentil soup and heated the contents on the stove, and then served it carefully, with fresh bread from a local bakery. He was trying. Hard, even. But I'd taken one look at the empty cans on the kitchen counter and known I couldn't possibly swallow any of their contents.

It was just the two of us. After a sharp "I hope you've pulled yourself together, Frances," Bubbe had retired to her room to watch television. I wondered how long I would have to stay. An hour? An hour and a half?

My father had put on some instrumental jazz. The music pulsed and strummed. I pretended to eat, and noticed after a while that my father was only pretending too. Head bowed, he was carefully ripping a slice of bread into smaller and smaller bits. Finally he placed a bite-size chunk in his mouth and proceeded to chew as if his jaw were made of glass. His Adam's apple bobbled when he finally swallowed. He drank the tiniest sip of water.

He stole a glance at me and, seeing that I was watching him, shot his gaze down again quickly. I stared at the thinning hair on top of his head. His scalp was shiny beneath the strands.

He was fifty years old. He lived with his mother. He wrote books nobody wanted to publish. His wife had left, his son had died, his daughter had nothing to say to him, or he to her.

Sadness for him – for us – welled up within me. I thought of his books. He was an interesting man, my father. He was a smart man. So, why? Why?

I didn't know.

We listened to the jazz. And then I found myself saying quietly: "Dad? Can I ask your opinion about something?"

He looked up, seeming relieved that I'd spoken, but also wary. "Yes?"

I had spent hours turning the afternoon at the food pantry over in my mind, not understanding anything beyond the indisputable fact that I felt itchy, troubled. I'd wondered briefly about talking to Ms Wiles, but we had already had this conversation, she and I.

"It's about Patrick Leyden," I said to my father.

He nodded. "The Internet guy."

"Yes. You know he's active at Pettengill and with the Unity charity group that Daniel was part of? He was even here at the house…" I paused. *When we sat shivah for Daniel.*

My father nodded. "Yes."

I rushed on. "I just wondered – I know you don't really know him, but you follow technology trends, and new companies, and science stuff. And Daniel—" I stumbled over the name. "Daniel talked about him, and you did meet him and everything. And well, I just wondered what you think of him. What your opinion is."

"My opinion," said my father.

"Yes." And then impulsively I added: "Ms Wiles – that's my art teacher, you know – says he's a dickhead." Childishly, I had wanted to say that word in front of my father, but he didn't blink. I went on. "But she also says that he does a lot of good in the world, and that matters more."

There was a short silence. My father was looking at me through his glasses thoughtfully. He looked almost professorial, and when he spoke, his voice was strong. Interested. He said, "And what do you think of Patrick Leyden, Frances?"

I found I was squirming. "Well, Daniel really adored him. Thought he was kind of a God. But I think..."

"He's a dickhead?" said my father. To my astonishment a smile had formed on his lips.

"Yes," I said. "But I don't know. Maybe that's necessary in order to be a success in business. That kind of thing."

"So they say," said my father dryly. We looked at each other. I found I was smiling a little as well.

"'The rich are different from you and me'," quoted my father. "F. Scott Fitzgerald. Although Hemingway then replied, 'Yes. They have more money.'" He shrugged. "I don't know, Frances. Do you want to have an abstract discussion about wealth and corruption? We could do that – I'm happy to – but I'll tell you up front that my opinion probably has more than a tinge of sour grapes to it. As you might expect, given my general level of success in life." He ducked his head again suddenly, but then looked up and met my eyes straight on.

Discomfort washed over me. My father's frankness was difficult to hear.

He went on: "The fact is, one tries not to want what one doesn't have. One tends to think it's valueless."

Not exactly, I thought. Lots of people want and value *only* what they don't have. Then: *Daniel*, I thought, with sudden recognition. *Daniel*.

My father was studying his hands. His shoulders were braced. I had a simultaneous urge to end the conversation immediately – to flee – and to continue. I shifted in my chair. And then my father said slowly, "I had this conversation with your brother once."

"What?" I leaned forward. "You mean you talked to Daniel about..."

"Patrick Leyden. Yes. Oh, he didn't ask my opinion. I just – offered it." My father's lips twisted. "I was glad about the scholarships for you two, but when your brother started in – Patrick Leyden this, Patrick Leyden that – I took him aside."

I was fascinated. "What did you say?"

"That a man like Leyden never does anything that doesn't benefit himself in some way. And that Dan- your brother should keep that in mind."

"And what did Daniel say?" I asked.

"He told me," said my father, "that he would remember." He

blinked at me ruefully. "He was quite polite, actually. He even said thank you. I wasn't sure it was my son for a minute there."

"When was this?"

"Your first year at Pettengill," said my father promptly. "Second semester."

"Huh," I said. It had been then that Daniel intensified his involvement with Unity.

"Frances?" said my father.

"What?"

"Um. Are you in danger of getting a crush on Patrick Leyden, like your brother?"

"No!" A vision of Leyden's earlobes invaded my brain, immediately overlaid with another, of James's smile. "Absolutely not!"

"Good," said my father. He fiddled with his spoon. "Then take his scholarship and run, Frances. Don't look this particular gift horse in the mouth until *after* graduation. That's my advice."

We slipped back into our accustomed silence. It felt a little easier between us. And when I stood up to go and my father asked, as he always did, if he could drive me back to school, for once I said yes. And then, before getting out of the car, I added, "Thanks, Dad."

He replied diffidently, "Sure."

We didn't kiss or hug. We hadn't done those things since I was nine. But I felt his eyes follow me, through the window of his old car, as I walked without looking back to the door of my dorm.

23

It was only nine o'clock. Walking through the dorm on my way to my room, I could feel the taut quiet that defined end-of-weekend study panic at Pettengill. Aline Subramanya had put a big sign on her door: I AM IN CHINA DURING THE YÜAN DYNASTY. ON PAIN OF BLOODY TORTURE AND DEATH, DO NOT DISTRUB. It was typical of Aline to have put the umlaut in Yüan. I shook my head, but also felt a pang of envy. China, centuries ago – that sounded pretty good right now. And I could almost imagine that if you did open Aline's door, you'd find yourself stepping into a mysterious, long-ago world.

Who knew, in fact, what was behind any of the doors in the dorm? What if the doors were portals, of the kind my father might write about in a science fiction novel? What if each of them took you into a place defined only by the occupant's mind?

What would my father put in his world? The oracle? Death? What would George de Witt, or Pammy Rosenfeld or Tonia Mack from art class? I tried to imagine Saskia's world, and winced. And, of course, the world I wanted – no, longed – to know about belonged to—

James Droussian.

In that moment I understood that the thought of James had been with me all day. He had been a swift, silent current running beneath everything that happened, behind everything I did and said and heard. All day, yes, and last night too, beneath my sleep and my dreams. James, James, James. Wondering where he was, and what he was doing, and what he was thinking – and if his thoughts could possibly be of me.

Reaching my room, going inside with the usual relief – *my* world – I felt my whole being flood with the secret, guilty joy of letting myself think of him. Even though somewhere in me, mixed in with my quickened pulse, I knew it was quite hopeless, because—

I grabbed my elbows, suddenly overwhelmed by the memory of how James had looked at me in the cafeteria after I threw my plate and had the hysterical laughing fit. After he'd slapped me. In his expression, in his eyes... I recognised now what I'd seen there, and there was no sense pretending it wasn't what it was.

Pity.

I sat down on the edge of my bed.

Some time passed; I don't know how long. Eventually I looked vaguely round my room. I looked at the mourning-draped mirror, and for some reason my gaze stayed there.

I knew I'd put it up to remind me of Daniel's death, to remind me of my failure to be a good sister, to remind me of how much I hadn't known. But somehow those reasons seemed murky to me now.

Jews put black over mirrors during times of mourning so they wouldn't think about themselves. But I never did look in mirrors anyway, because I disliked myself. No, wait. I disliked my appearance.

I felt so confused. So much around me, and in me, seemed to have changed – and all in the past several days. Yet none of it made any sense to me. It seemed as if there were all kinds of things that I *almost* knew – that I *should* know, but didn't. And if I could know them, could drag them into consciousness and understand them, all would be well.

Or maybe not. Daniel would still be dead.

Attention leads to immortality. Carelessness leads to death.

I curled myself into a knot on my bed and tried to think of nothing at all.

Later I heaved myself up, determined to stop feeling sorry for myself – and study, dammit. Ms Wiles would approve of that. And there was certainly plenty to do. I even had a list. Somewhere.

I found the list. Research for a paper on, yes, something to do with China. Figure out how to program an applet into a web page. Learn the molecular structure of gases. And read that novel *Beloved*, about which an essay was due next week.

I couldn't imagine attempting to do any of the active studying, so I opened the novel. I read the first page, and then the second. On the third I realised I couldn't recall a word. I closed the book. I got up and paced the small confines of my room. James – no. No.

I hated Sunday nights. They always felt melancholy. I got up and turned off the overhead light, leaving on only the bedside lamp on top of the nightstand. The nightstand. There was a little weed left in Mr Monkey, I knew. Enough for a cigarette or two. I sat on my bed and took out Mr Monkey. I held his little plastic body in my hands and looked at his silly expression.

That itchy feeling I had had earlier came back. It whispered that I *still* wasn't paying enough attention.

I tore off Mr Monkey's head and hurled it across the room. Unlike the plate the other day, Mr Monkey's head bounced against the wall. It rolled back again, landing nearly at my feet.

OK, I wasn't getting something, but there was nothing I could do about it. I wasn't the Buddha. I couldn't have a vision. Unless, maybe, it was drug-induced.

Yeah, right. Like the other night, when I'd dreamed of Daniel as the Buddha. One stupid question. That had been helpful. Sure.

I reached for Mr Monkey's head and fitted him back together. Then I put him away. I did not smoke the remaining marijuana.

I looked at the bedside clock. Too late to call Ms Wiles and describe what I'd overheard at the pantry this afternoon. Too late to ask her opinion. And besides, Ms Wiles... Another itchy thought flitted through my mind and then was gone.

The room was dim. The black-draped mirror was only a shadow on the wall now. I rose and went to it. I stood in front of it. With one fingertip I traced a fold in the fabric.

I thought of Snow White's stepmother and her truth-telling mirror. The stepmother had asked only about beauty – and it wasn't that I blamed her. I understood her yearning and I wondered, in fact, if that stepmother had been an unattractive young woman before she blossomed into her queenly self.

What if a mirror really did have the power to show you what was beneath the surface? What if it were like Picasso?

What if it showed you your soul?

My hand reached out. I removed the black silk. I stared into the dim, unfamiliar reflection. Vaguely I could see the line of my brow. The bulk of my hair. My face only, not my body. That was safer. Mirror, mirror, on the wall...

No. I turned away.

Then I turned back.

I looked, not straight at my face, but at its components. First I skimmed my gaze over my hair. Its thick texture was one of the things that told people I couldn't be wholly Asian. But how had I managed not to notice that it had got so long? That it stood out around my head with a frizzy life of its own? It was pretty hair, I thought, unable to repress a spurt of vanity. Even if it didn't fit with my Asian features, even if it wasn't straight and silky. Maybe if I brushed it more often... I couldn't help it; I reached up tentatively and tried holding it up, in a bun kind of thing. It looked fine that way.

And it made my cheekbones stick out. I looked at those cheekbones, noting their sharpness. When had my face stopped being chubby? Where had those slight hollows in the cheeks come from? And my skin was smooth, dark. Like Sayoko's.

Then, turning my head, I saw that the ear – my ear – was slightly pointed, delicate. Bizarre! My hair had always covered my ears. I examined the other one. Yes, they were a pair of alien ears; I had never looked at them before. And my eyebrows!

Straight dark lines that angled a bit upwards towards my temples, matching the ears somehow.

But then I examined my nose and grimaced. Like my hair, my nose announced that I wasn't all of one piece. My nose had a high bridge. In fact, I knew that nose! It was Bubbe's, right in the middle of my face, sneering in familiar haughty disapproval.

My gaze travelled down quickly to my mouth. A second ago it had almost smiled, but now it had returned to the expression that I suspected was its normal state. It was drawn-in, tight, careful. Bitter? I tried to make it smile again, but it wasn't having any of that.

Round chin. Boring, but OK.

Lastly, finally, I looked at – but not into – my eyes. Of course: dark-lashed, dark-hued. Tilted slightly to match the brows. Ordinary Asian eyes, I thought. Not large, not small. Fine. And, like the mouth, like all of it: unfamiliar.

There. I had taken inventory. I possessed all the usual features, located in all the usual places. Some I liked, some I didn't. I took a deep breath. It was time to step back and look at the whole face. To see... me. Frances.

Frances the mongrel. Frances the dwarf.

I straightened my shoulders. I had a wild thought that maybe this would be like the final page of a fairy tale, and I would discover that I had become beautiful. Duckling into swan. As beautiful in my way as Saskia was in hers.

I poked out my undistinguished chin, raised my imperious nose, drew in my brows, and then I looked. I really looked at the girl in the mirror.

She looked straight back at me.

She was not beautiful. She was not even pretty. But she – that girl with her combination features and suspicious mouth – was interesting-looking. She was someone that I, the artist, would have looked at twice. Would have wondered about.

The truly shocking thing was that I felt no kinship with her. I honestly felt no connection with her whatsoever.

Simultaneously, I and the girl in the mirror both put one hand up and touched a cheek.

Then, tentatively, I put both my hands on my body. Lightly, slowly – very differently from the mindless, efficient way I scrubbed with a washcloth when showering – I ran my hands from my shoulders to my knees. Breasts, ribcage, waist. Hips, butt, thighs. Even to my artist's hands, nothing felt... disproportionate. Not any more. Although of course, to be certain, I'd have to look. This mirror was small, but perhaps if I stood on a chair... tried to see what was really there... what I really did look like...

I turned away sharply from the mirror. I discovered that I was sitting on the edge of my bed. And for a second it was as if I'd transported back seven years and was sitting once more on the toilet lid in Bubbe's upstairs bathroom. Not daring to take off my clothes and look at my precocious nine-year-old body. Not daring – even now, at sixteen – to look at the poor freaky kid.

You are not going to be a dainty Japanese woman.

I got up again. I put the black silk over the mirror. I didn't look in at her – at me – while I did it. And the second that the mirror was decently covered again, I felt better.

24

The next few days were so ordinary that it seemed almost as if I'd dropped into a time warp and mysteriously returned to Pettengill in the days before Daniel died. But the ordinariness now felt false, mask-like.

I still had that feeling, the one that had grown on me so slowly, so inexorably. The feeling of waiting. The feeling that something just out of the periphery of my comprehension was badly wrong, and that I knew, somewhere in me, what it was.

There was a new sensation too. This one was extremely strange after all the years of being invisible. It was the feeling of being watched.

I knew I wasn't making it up. I caught people at it. My teachers, of course; I supposed that was only natural after my little tantrum in the cafeteria. Maybe it was also natural that the other kids would give me sidelong, half-wary, half-fascinated glances as well. *Will she, won't she, crack up?* Saskia shot me occasional fierce, frowning looks across the room in history. And Ms Wiles – she was worried, I knew.

I felt guilty about Ms Wiles. On Monday, when she'd

approached me with questions about how I was and what I'd thought of the Unity food pantry, I'd found myself brushing her off. I wasn't even sure why. "I'm fine," I'd said. "Yeah, it was OK at the food pantry. I have another shift on Thursday. But I have to go now, OK?"

She'd put a hand on my arm. "All right, Frances. Would you like to come over for tea this afternoon?"

"I can't," I'd said, even though I could have. I'd watched Ms Wiles's mouth drop open. I had never before refused one of her invitations to tea. I opened my own mouth to retract my refusal, but found myself saying, instead: "Bye. See you later."

No, I wasn't making up the eyes that followed me, judged me, wondered about me. But meanwhile, the one person whose eyes on me I would have welcomed – James – was nowhere to be found. I looked fruitlessly for him everywhere I went. At the same time, however, the bare possibility that I might see James added light and colour and texture to the world. There was potential every time I turned my head. I felt irradiated by it.

And then Thursday night, after an innocuous two hours of stacking dusty cans of beetroot and mushrooms at the Unity food pantry (with George de Witt, who wouldn't say more than two syllables the whole time), I was called into the office to meet, alone, with Patrick Leyden.

One more little weirdness: as I climbed up off my hands and knees to follow the summons, I thought – no, I was sure – that I heard George mutter beneath his breath: "Oh, Christ, no." But when I looked at him, he had his back to me, so I shrugged and followed Pammy to the office.

"There you are, Frances," said Patrick Leyden from behind the desk. He consulted his watch. "Have a seat. I can give this about ten minutes. Pammy," – she was lingering behind me – "you can close the door on your way out."

I heard the door close. I sat down on the edge of the chair opposite the desk, and was unable to repress a swift memory of Bubbe, years ago, mocking Daniel and me: *Look at you two, sitting right on the edge of your chairs. Ready to run!* Daniel, defiant, had responded by sliding his butt back firmly into the kitchen chair and glaring at her. But I had stayed exactly where I was, with my feet on the floor. Ready to run.

Now I wondered if, of the two reactions, mine hadn't in fact been the more defiant.

I had my feet on the floor now as well. I looked at Patrick Leyden. I stuck out my nose that was so like Bubbe's. You could say this for Bubbe: she appeared to fear nothing and no one. "What's up?" I said boldly.

Patrick Leyden raised a sarcastic eyebrow. "This is about the fundraising campaign, Frances. The Daniel Leventhal Memorial Fund Drive. Didn't I tell you we'd need to talk about that?"

"Oh," I said. "Right." But I hadn't realised it would be this soon. I squirmed, feeling a little less bold. I hated this memorial thing as much as ever.

"Well then," said Patrick Leyden briskly. "I explained the parameters of the situation and what I wanted to one of the people in my marketing department, and she was kind enough to prepare a letter that will go out over your signature. This will be the central mailing piece of the capital campaign. I'm sure you'll agree that it's a good job."

He held out a sheet of paper towards me.

I could feel my lips compressing into a tight line, but I took the letter. It was printed on Unity letterhead.

Dear Friend,

Not long ago my brother, Daniel, took a deliberate overdose of heroin – and with it, his own life. Daniel was funny and smart. He could have become someone wonderful. Instead, he is dead. He was seventeen years old.

I loved my brother and I mourn his passing. But I am also angry that Daniel made a decision that hurt his family and friends so much. I am angry at the waste of his potential. And I am angry because I know that my brother was only one of many young people who lose their way to drugs and despair. Who lack vision for the future.

I am writing to you because I believe that, if we try, we can help teens like Daniel. I believe we can fight drugs, death, and despair. And win.

As a friend of Unity Service, you probably know that Unity has been cited by the President of the United States, on the occasion of the award of a Presidential Freedom Medal, as a "shining beacon to teens everywhere, proving that it's possible for positive action by young people to impact not only the local, but the national community". (See enclosed reprint of *Time* magazine article.) Our network of charity programmes is well known and has received extensive praise (see enclosed brochure).

The brightest light in Unity's beacon is our scholarship

programme, which began right here at The Pettengill School, where I am a student. The programme has since spread to excellent preparatory schools all over the country. Nearly two hundred underprivileged teenagers today now have access to the best possible secondary education. This education is intended to provide the foundation for long, happy, productive futures.

We in Unity Service have therefore begun this capital campaign so that we can expand the scholarship programme down to middle schools. We do this for teens like my brother, who began using drugs when he was eleven—

There were several paragraphs more, but my head snapped up without reading them. I'd been growing steadily more sickened, but this was the worst. "This is a lie! Daniel wasn't using drugs at eleven!"

"Yes," said Patrick Leyden evenly. "He was. He told me so."

I gritted my teeth. I looked back down at the letter as if I was reading on, but I didn't do so. No. I remembered when Daniel was eleven, and this I would not buy.

My father's words came back to me. What was in this for Patrick Leyden?

Pretend work.

The dusty cans...

A voice in my head was screaming at me. *You know. You know. You know!*

Wallace's voice as he talked with Pammy. *They* are *our partners, you know... All the customers need to be reimbursed.*

"Well?" Patrick Leyden said impatiently. "There should be no surprises in the letter. I'm particularly pleased about the associated website. That was a good thought; people can just charge their contributions online. Maybe we'll move that information from the bottom to nearer the top of the letter. Or add it to the letterhead. Or both."

I didn't say anything. A disembodied terror had gripped me. I folded the letter in two, carefully creasing it.

"I see," said Patrick Leyden. "You're still being childish about this, Frances. I thought you'd had a change of heart."

I remembered the way I'd felt when I'd first learned that Daniel was dead. My – incredulity.

Daniel wouldn't have done it. Daniel wouldn't have killed himself. But Saskia had known Daniel better than I did, and she'd had no doubt that he'd killed himself... had she? It was to Saskia that Daniel had addressed his final letter...

Daniel, in my dream, shaking his head. No, no, no.

Dread filled me. I could taste it, acid, at the back of my throat. I didn't want to know.

As my silence – and my staring – continued, Patrick Leyden grew red in the face. "You do understand that I don't need you for this? The letter could easily be rewritten in the third person. We're going to do this capital campaign with or without you."

And then suddenly I could talk. I was myself. I was present. I looked at Patrick Leyden and said, "Yes. I understand that."

"Then make up your mind. If you want to be part of this

organisation, you will help this organisation in whichever way I see fit. Otherwise – you're out."

"I'm just going to think about it for another day," I said calmly, and got up. "I'll get back to you, Mr Leyden."

Patrick Leyden began speaking – perhaps it was sputtering – but I ignored him. I walked out. I left. Andy Jankowski had taught me how.

Andy.

Outside the office, things had slowed down. End of shift. End of night. I looked round. George and Pammy were talking over by the clothing area. Most of the lights had been switched off.

Are you here to do pretend work too, Frances Leventhal?

I think they're going to have me pack cans of vegetables.

Pretend, yes. All fake work.

I discovered that even though I didn't understand anything, I absolutely knew what I should do right now.

I went and found Andy. He was sitting by the entrance, a faraway expression on his face. I waved as I approached, and he waved back.

"Hello, Frances Leventhal," Andy said. I thought he looked pleased to see me.

"Hey," I answered. As ever, I felt something in me soften and relax in his presence. I said awkwardly, "Andy, I was wondering if you would walk back to Pettengill with me. After you finish up here? I need an escort, and I'd like to talk to you about something. If that's OK with you."

Andy sat up. He looked solemn. "Frances Leventhal, that is no problem. I am a very good escort."

"Thanks," I said.

"And," said Andy, shyly, but with something a little defiant in his voice as well, "I have something to tell you."

25

It was cold outside again, but the temperature was not too much below freezing. Pammy and George had seemed incredulous when we declined a lift in the van, but it wasn't bad if you kept moving. I had Daniel's scarf wrapped round my head and ears, and my mittens on, with my hands stuffed in my pockets for good measure. Andy was bareheaded but seemed indifferent to the temperature, except for offering me his coat with some persistence.

"Really, I'm fine," I said. "This is a warm coat. And I promise I'll tell you if I get cold."

"You'll tell me?"

"I'll tell you."

"OK," he said finally.

We walked briskly in silence for a few steps, while I tried to think of a clear way to ask Andy why he'd implied that stacking cans was as much pretend work as watching the door. But before I could formulate the question, Andy forestalled me. Again with that hint of defiance in his voice – and, I thought, some excitement – he said, "I checked,

Frances Leventhal. And it *is* all pretend work. All of it!"

My head swung sharply to the side. In the street lamps, I could only see the shadow of Andy's profile, but he was nearly bouncing with emotion: indignation? Affronted pride? "What?" I said. "You checked? What do you mean?"

"I checked the boxes again," Andy said. "They were stacked by the door. And they're still the same. Always the same old boxes, packed with the same stuff. Carry in, carry out. It's fake work. I already knew. But I checked today while you were there, and yesterday, and the day before that. There's no real work. It's the same old boxes, Frances Leventhal! Always the same old boxes!"

Andy paused. I felt my heart rate increase. What Andy was saying – it still didn't make sense to me, but the feeling that I knew, I *knew*, intensified.

"Something is very wrong at that food pantry." It popped out of my mouth. I couldn't believe I'd let myself say that in front of Andy, but—

He smiled at me. I could see the gleam of his teeth in the darkness. "You didn't understand me the other day," he said with satisfaction. "You thought packing the cans was real work. I could tell. So I checked."

"Huh," I said. I found myself remembering how dirty the "newly-arrived" cans had been. My hands had got filthy, unpacking and stacking them. Would new donations be that dusty, right out of the box? Well, maybe some, but *all* of the cans? I felt that flickering lightbulb struggling, again, to come on above my head.

"Do you understand what I'm saying now?" Andy demanded. We had hastened our pace a little, and were hunched against the wind.

"I'm getting there," I said grimly. "Explain again about the same old boxes."

It took nearly the whole walk – Andy got tangled up as he talked – but I listened intently, and eventually I figured out what he'd been struggling to say. Why he thought the work at the pantry was "fake".

Why he was right.

Andy had come to recognise the two dozen or so cardboard boxes that came and went, every couple of days, from the food pantry. The one with the battered corner, the one that said "Green Giant #1890065279" (Andy recited the numbers precisely), the one with part of its top flap ripped away. A box would get replaced from time to time, as it broke, but for the most part the same boxes were used over and over. Each box would leave the pantry full of stuff, securely sealed with packing tape – and then return a day or two later, still sealed with the same packing tape.

"Same boxes. Same contents. Into the van one day. Out of the van the next," Andy said. "Fake work. Waste of time."

"Maybe the boxes are just being recycled?" I ventured. "And the contents have changed?" But as soon as I'd said it, I shook my head. It didn't make sense to work that way. Why would you pack up and seal new donations into boxes, when they were just headed for the warehouse to be sorted and stacked and so on? And why wouldn't you leave the boxes with the families who were supposed to get them?

"Andy, you say the boxes come back still sealed, the same way they went out. And they weigh the same?"

"They weigh the same." Andy sounded very pleased with himself. "I can tell. And the packing tape hasn't been changed. It looks the same as before. The same stuff must be inside. Does that make sense, Frances Leventhal?"

"Yes," I said slowly. "It makes sense..."

I thought of all the things I'd seen at the pantry. Heaps of things. Shoes, clothing, toys. I burst out incredulously, "So wait. Nobody's getting anything, then? No families are getting toys or cans or clothes? And nobody's giving any of those things to the pantry? The same items cycle in and out? Pretend donations? Pretend charity?"

Andy frowned. "I don't know. I just know it's fake work."

At that exact moment the lightbulb above my head stopped flickering; it came on and stayed on.

I wet my lips. I could feel my heart begin to pound. "It's a front," I said hoarsely. "The Unity food pantry is a front." Presidential Freedom Medal. Biggest student charitable concern in the country. The same boxes. Carry in, carry out. No charitable deliveries. No charitable donations. Fake work.

It wasn't just one bulb above my head now. It was a whole sound-and-light show.

Unity was a front.

26

"What's a front?" asked Andy.

It took me a minute to focus on his question. Other bits of knowledge were snaking through my bloodstream, threatening to paralyse me. Daniel – shaking his head in my dream. That lying letter of Patrick Leyden's. The fact that Daniel's note had been to Saskia. What I really did, and really didn't, know about my brother...

I searched for words, soothing words that would hold off that darkness a little longer. I said slowly to Andy, "A front is a business operation that isn't what it seems to be. Like, for example, a store that sells refrigerators, but their true business is something illegal like, oh, counterfeiting money in the back room, or – or selling drugs." I felt my mittened hand go to my mouth, but it was too late.

I stopped walking. I stood on the sidewalk and, abruptly, ceased to fight a battle I hadn't even realised I was waging. I let a geyser of sounds and images swell up within me.

I let myself know what I knew.

When's she going to figure out that it's easier to do speed than throw up? Maybe somebody should ease her in with some diet pills. Wallace Chan to James, my love, the small-time drug dealer, at that Pettengill meeting. *I can't believe you'd seriously presume to lecture us about ethics.* The irony of it...

My subterranean feeling – for days, weeks, no, years – that lots of people – Daniel, Saskia, James – knew something I didn't.

Saskia's jewellery and clothes.

My wild musings about James running a drug empire at a prep school because the customers and money were plentiful.

As if I were operating a kaleidoscope, the things I'd seen or heard or knew whirled round and round and then settled into a complex but perfectly symmetrical pattern.

All these thoughts took only a few seconds. Meanwhile Andy had gone on a step or two, but then had turned back for me. "Frances Leventhal?" I was vaguely aware of him as he put out a hand and caught my arm. "Are you all right, Frances Leventhal?"

I was still looking at the pattern. It was not unlike the paintings on the walls of my room; obscured, but clear to anyone who took the time to see. And I might be slow, but in the end I always recognise when a picture speaks truth.

Even – or especially – when it's ugly.

Unity Service was a front for a prep school drug-dealing operation. And Daniel had been involved with them. He was no innocent, but—

I felt my lips move. "They killed my brother," I whispered.

"What?" said Andy. He had both hands on my shoulders

now. He was holding me upright. His hands tightened a little in anxiety, and somehow the feel of them brought me back to myself a little. His voice rose. "Frances Leventhal, what did you say. What about your brother?"

All at once I realised that I couldn't get Andy tangled up in this... in this... whatever it was. And I was crazy! Daniel had killed himself – taken an overdose. There was no reason to leap to another conclusion. "Never mind," I managed. "I'm sorry. I just – just..." I couldn't think what to say.

I wanted – I couldn't – I didn't know – couldn't assimilate—

I didn't know what to do. I couldn't think. The police – I had to tell the police – but what about James – was he involved?— No! He couldn't be. My brother – my father – Saskia – I couldn't think—

Andy was looking down into my face. "You're pale, Frances Leventhal. You're sick again. I heard you were in the infirmary."

"No, I'm not sick now..." I said. But I did feel sick.

A deep wrinkle cut straight across Andy's forehead. "It's only a few minutes back to Pettengill. I can take you to the nurse." His expression brightened. "I'll carry you there. I'm very strong." Before I could say anything, he stooped and all at once was carrying me in his arms, walking carefully, his face anxious. "Only five minutes," he said. "Are you warm enough, Frances Leventhal? Say something!"

I wanted to say that I could walk, but I didn't. "I'm warm," I said confusedly. "I'm OK. I don't want the nurse."

"You're sick again."

"No..."

Andy had told the truth; he was very strong. I felt his arms beneath my back and legs; I felt oddly secure. I knew he wouldn't drop me. My eyes squeezed shut. Where was my father? He never touched me.

I looped an arm around Andy's neck and held on, to make it easier for him to carry me.

"You are sick," said Andy definitely. "It's because of what I told you. About the boxes and the fake work. I'm sorry, Frances Leventhal. It's not important. I didn't want you to get sick. The nurse will make you better."

I opened my eyes. One thing stood out amid my confusion: I did not want to be taken to the nurse. The thought focused me, and I had a small brainstorm.

I said urgently, "Andy. I don't want the nurse, but could you take me to see Ms Wiles?"

Andy's steps slowed a little. "The art teacher?"

"Yes." I could hear the new strength in my voice. This was a brilliant idea; in fact, it was the only idea. "Yvette Wiles. Her cottage is near yours. She's not just a teacher, she's a friend of mine."

She was my friend. My friend who knew truth when she saw it, just like I did. My friend who'd called Patrick Leyden a dickhead. I could talk to Ms Wiles. She'd believe me when I explained everything to her, because she knew me. She was the only one who knew me.

"Oh," said Andy. Then, uncertainly: "Ms Wiles will help you?"

I could feel myself lightening. "She will." She would know what to do with the theory – the knowledge – that was filling me up like poison. She would know how I – how we – should act.

"OK, Frances Leventhal," said Andy. "If that is what you want, I will take you to Ms Wiles." I felt his stride widen a little. "Two minutes."

"Great," I said, and I could hear the relief in my voice, could feel my own too, all through my body.

Two minutes, and then I would no longer be alone.

27

From the sofa in Ms Wiles's living room, with a teacup between my cold hands and an afghan over my knees, I marvelled at how unaccustomed I was to being taken care of. "Lucky that I was making this big pot of stew," Ms Wiles called from the kitchen area. She turned and smiled at me. "We'll have a nice chat, just the two of us, and you can tell me what's got you so pale and weak-kneed. Then we'll eat my stew."

It sounded like heaven, even though I was now a little worried about how exactly I would explain my – what were they? Suspicions? – to Ms Wiles. My certainty that she would understand and believe me had faded in the ordinary warmth and sanity of her pretty cottage. It was very possible that she would think I was dramatising, overreacting.

"Did you notice how I had to work to make Andy go home?" Ms Wiles continued. "He seems to be very fond of you, Frances."

Was there something weird in her tone? I put my teacup down carefully. "I like Andy," I said. "He's a nice man. He's *kind*. You saw how he helped me. We're – I guess we're sort of becoming friends."

"Ah," said Ms Wiles.

I found I'd clenched my hands together. A string of sentences formed instantly and forcefully in my mind. *Retarded or not, I like Andy Jankowski better than anyone I know. And I bet he's lonely! You might not know what that is, but I do. Would it have killed you to offer him a cup of tea too? You practically pushed him out the door!*

Tears pressed at my eyelids. I didn't let them fall. I was appalled at my own thoughts. I wanted to talk to Ms Wiles alone, didn't I? Wasn't I glad she'd got rid of Andy? And surely I was imagining that she was implying something nasty about my newly-budding friendship with him.

Andy needs a friend, I thought fiercely, protectively. He needs a good, reliable friend. Later, I thought, when this is all over – I shied away from what exactly I meant by "this" – I'll be his friend.

But right now, I knew, I needed Ms Wiles, not Andy. I looked round the room, at all of Ms Wiles's lovely idiosyncratic things. I looked at the closed door of her sunporch studio. I remembered how much we had in common, how she had always understood me, how akin our souls were. I remembered what she'd said about Patrick Leyden. She would believe me. She would help me. I would tell her my story, and we would eat her stew, and then we would go to the police together.

I sipped more tea and tried to relax, and Ms Wiles came by with the teapot and poured me more, and then took a seat at the other end of the sofa and tucked her feet up under herself. "Now, Frances," she said, and her pretty face was somehow both calm and concerned. "Tell me everything."

I took a deep breath. Then I said bluntly to her: "I think that

Unity isn't a real charity, Ms Wiles. I think it's a front for a drug distribution ring. Students are involved, and some adults too. Patrick Leyden. He runs it, obviously." I thought of the conversation I'd overheard between Wallace and Pammy. "And there's alumni involvement too. I don't know how it works, exactly. But I have some pieces, and I can guess."

Ms Wiles's mouth had dropped open. She was staring at me and I couldn't read her thoughts.

"Do you think I'm crazy?" I asked. "I'm not. I know this is true. I know it! And even if I am crazy, it won't hurt to tell the police all this. Let me explain more."

Finally Ms Wiles reacted. She took a deep breath, shaking her head minutely, and then managed to smile. She said simply: "You astonish me, Frances. In more ways than you know. OK. Go on. Explain."

And my heart filled with gratitude.

She didn't interrupt me, and after a couple of minutes I wasn't really even talking to her any more, I was talking to myself. I jumped up and began pacing the room. I was thinking aloud, feeling more and more pieces slot in as I talked. Everything just poured out of me.

Suppose you're Patrick Leyden. You're a teenager, and a student at Pettengill, and you're smart. You see that drug use is rampant at your school. There are lots of rich kids with money to spend and the inclination to spend it, and the police are busy stomping on drugs in the inner city, not in the educational institutions of the wealthy and privileged.

Relatively speaking, a place like Pettengill is actually kind of a safe place to buy and sell drugs. Everyone knows it's happening, and everyone turns a blind eye. The adults say it's just marijuana. Just steroids. Just diet pills. Oh, and a few designer pills sometimes, and a little coke, but that's it. Kids will be kids. Everybody's sophisticated, nobody really gets hurt, and God forbid there should be bad publicity that will damage the school's reputation, upset the alumni, and discourage parents from enrolling their kids. So, as long as things are quiet, nobody does much to discourage what's going on.

You see all this, and you realise that you could deal drugs yourself in a small way – "like James Droussian," I said, and saw Ms Wiles's eyes flicker – but you have bigger ambitions. You figure that what goes on at one prep school goes on at another. You think, why should I make a small sum when, if I set things up properly, I could make really big bucks?

So you decide to create an organisation.

"A secret organisation?" said Ms Wiles from her end of the sofa.

"A front," I said again, impatiently. "A secret that looks like it's not a secret. That's what Unity is. A drug distribution network masquerading as a charitable organisation, with its day-to-day business run by the poor students who took scholarships from the organisation. Kids like Saskia. And —" I stuttered " – and my brother. Poor kids, looking for a way to fit in. Not that it would be only poor kids dealing – Unity has lots of regular kids too. But the poor kids are the vulnerable ones... and they wouldn't need to openly deal. Not all of them. Not even most of them. There must be all kinds of jobs involved in a big operation like this."

"And you think that Patrick Leyden conceived all this when he was a teenager himself?"

"Yes," I said. "He started Unity back when he was a student. And he's stayed involved all these years. It adds up. It all makes sense."

"He doesn't need drug money," Ms Wiles remarked. "He has his Internet company, Cognitive Reach. It's very successful."

"He started Cognitive Reach with drug money," I said excitedly. "I'm sure of it. I mean – I don't *know*, but it would make sense." I sank back on to the sofa. "Listen, Ms Wiles, Daniel was obsessed with Patrick Leyden. He read all the news and background information he could find on him and on Cognitive Reach. He was always talking about him. And I remember – I think I remember – there were several anonymous 'angel' investors in the early stage of the company. They gave huge sums of money to get the company off the ground and their names were never revealed. And I'm betting that money was Patrick Leyden's Unity drug money, fronted by others." I stopped. I could read Ms Wiles's expression now, and it wasn't one of belief and engagement. "I know it sounds far-fetched," I said defensively. "And OK, I'm just guessing at pieces of this..."

In the silence, I could hear the ticking of Ms Wiles's hubcap clock. Then she said gently, "Is there any part of this that you're *not* guessing at?"

I swallowed. Suddenly the logical structure that had seemed so clear in my mind trembled and crumbled. I flailed around in the debris looking for something to say. Andy's testimony about the boxes! But there was the way Ms Wiles had spoken of Andy earlier – and somehow I didn't mention him now... a retarded man's testimony...

"Any part at all?" persisted Ms Wiles. "Any proof? Do you have *proof*, Frances?"

The dust on the cans at the food pantry. Saskia's clothes and jewellery. Even the way Daniel had tried so hard to alienate me – now it flew into my head to wonder if he'd been trying to protect me. Could it be?

I swallowed. "Ms Wiles, look. You don't have to believe it. I just thought, if you'd come to the police with me. Let them take over. Please. I just need you to support me while I tell someone – someone who can investigate properly."

The hubcap clock ticked on in the quiet.

I remembered something Saskia had said to me during her tour. *We act as a central clearing-house for donations and redistribution. Of course, these days we're pushing people to donate plain cash. That way we can buy what's most needed, and not be stuck redistributing useless stuff that people really ought to throw out.* Money, I thought despairingly. If only I'd been as interested as Daniel in money and how it works, I might have done a better job of piecing this together.

"You're a very creative girl, Frances," Ms Wiles said finally. "Smart too. A little overwhelmed, though, and very, very sad and lonely. It's maybe not surprising that you've let your imagination run away with you..."

I stared at her. My brain whipped desperately on. Patrick Leyden's marketing campaign to expand the scholarship programme to middle schools – if I was right, he was planning to move his drug distribution operation in among the littler kids...

"I like you very much, Frances," said Ms Wiles gently. "But the other day you nearly had a breakdown, sweetheart. I think you're imagining things now. After all," she repeated, "it's not as if you have any proof."

"No," I said. "No, I'm not imagining anything." But I knew it was useless. *They killed my brother.* I felt the words well up wildly inside me. *Ms Wiles, they killed Daniel! I know it!* But I didn't let the thought escape. I knew it wouldn't be believed. And she was right: I had no proof.

"So you won't go with me to the police?" I said.

Ms Wiles got up. "We're going to have my nice stew," she said. "And after that, Frances, I'm going to walk you to the infirmary. You can get a good night's sleep there, and then we'll talk tomorrow." She paused. "I'd really like to believe you, Frances. If you just had something concrete – but you don't, do you?"

Helplessly I shook my head.

Ms Wiles shook hers back. "Then it's hard not to think you're a little... well, delusional."

She smiled kindly. Very kindly.

28

If I'd thought things through, I wouldn't have done what I did next, because there was really no point to it. It wasn't as if I were thinking of actually running away – from Pettengill, from Lattimore. But as I sat bewildered and unbelieved in Ms Wiles's living room, defiance filled me. I wasn't going to let Ms Wiles take me to the nurse like a – like a kicked kitten.

Ms Wiles was in the kitchen, ladling out stew, saying something that I didn't bother to hear. Intending simply to slip out, I quietly crossed the room towards the front door, grabbing my coat as I passed. But my gaze fixed itself on the door to Ms Wiles's studio, and I found I'd approached it and grasped the knob. It turned easily. The room was unlocked.

Then, as if I'd planned it, I found myself swivelling back to the front door, silently opening it a few inches, and then turning back to step inside the studio and close that door behind me.

And there, finally inside the studio that I'd longed to see ever since I'd known Ms Wiles, I froze in shock. It wasn't completely dark in the room – some light filtered in round the window blinds – but it wasn't possible to see very well either. That didn't matter, though. I had no need to use my eyes.

I inhaled sharply. Behind me I could hear Ms Wiles's exclamation, hear her running feet as she crossed the living room to the open front door. Hear her call after me – she thought – into the winter dark: "Frances! Frances, come back!"

None of this mattered. Standing in the converted sunporch, my nose and lungs telegraphed information directly to my brain.

The room smelled wrong. There was no charcoal or graphite dust in the air. No rich lingering stench of turpentine or oil. No tiny fruity aroma of a recently-used acrylic. No dirty or damp or dried-out rags. There was not even – artwork aside – the normal human scent that any well-used room takes on. And, finally, the place was bitterly cold.

Ms Wiles had never created art in this room. No one had, ever.

It was very nearly empty. A few boxes were stacked against one wall, but that was it.

I slipped my arms into the sleeves of my coat and buttoned it. But... Ms Wiles *was* an artist, I reminded myself. She couldn't have fooled me about that – let alone have fooled the school, and all the other students. Ms Wiles taught art, and she taught it well. She knew what she was talking about. She understood what she saw. That wasn't faked. That *couldn't* be faked.

But none of it mattered right now, because even if Ms Wiles was a real artist with real work of her own, she didn't do that work here – and she had lied about it. So, what else might she have lied about? The answer leapt into my mind: *about being my friend.*

I exhaled slowly. I thought of how Ms Wiles had urged me to get involved with Unity. Urged me to cooperate with Patrick Leyden's grand campaign to raise money for middle-school scholarships.

When we were sitting shivah for Daniel, Ms Wiles had been talking with Patrick Leyden. She called him a dickhead to me, but he called her Yvette.

I found my way to a box in the corner of the false studio and sat on its edge. Patrick Leyden. Who *wasn't* he intimate with at Pettengill? All the Unity kids, the Pettengill alumni, people in the school administration – they all loved him. He donated money, he got great publicity. How many of them knew the truth about Unity? There were teachers who were involved with Unity explicitly. Some of them had been at the meeting I'd gone to. Who else had been there? The associate dean – oh, God. Where did it end? No one was safe for me to talk to. Anyone could be involved...

Vaguely I was aware that in the next room Ms Wiles had made a phone call or two. I couldn't make out her words – I didn't even try. I didn't cross to the door and press my ear against it. I didn't make plans or try to work anything out.

I just sat.

Ms Wiles.

And James, my James, who was not mine at all. I tried to tell myself that he was new to Pettengill, he was dealing in a small-time way, he was not, could not, be involved with Unity. But with despair I remembered the time I'd seen him in the woods with a strange man, and the furtiveness of it all, and I couldn't convince myself. If Ms Wiles could be involved, why not James? That scene at the meeting, when he'd confronted and angered Patrick Leyden – it might have been staged. Although I couldn't think why...

One thing I did know, though: I had a stupid heart. I loved the wrong people.

I forced my mind onward.

Daniel.

My brother. What had really happened to Daniel? The fleeting thought I'd had earlier came back inexorably. Daniel had been so vehement, so vicious, about not wanting me involved with Unity. I wondered again – was it at all possible that he had been trying to protect me? I so wanted to believe it. I tried to remember a single tender thing my brother had said to me since we began at Pettengill, since he'd joined Unity, since he'd become involved with Saskia.

But there was nothing.

Had Daniel been killed? Was it really not a suicide? My thoughts flew round and round like vultures circling a dying man. There was my dream, but that wasn't all I had to go on. Saskia and the Unity kids had been the only ones who could confirm that Daniel had been suicidal. Who could confirm his "longtime drug habit". My throat filled with the old hatred for Saskia. She'd claimed Daniel had written her that brief suicide note. What if he hadn't? What if Saskia had written it? What if Patrick Leyden had?

I thought of Saskia in her beautiful clothes. Maybe, if not for Saskia, Daniel would have joined me in disdaining Unity. Maybe—

But I couldn't fool myself about that for very long. Unity had not been about Saskia for Daniel. It had been about Patrick Leyden. Patrick Leyden had killed Daniel, if anyone had. Indirectly, at least – and maybe even directly.

Then my nails bit at my palms, and I thought, *What if they did kill Daniel? What's been done once is easier the second time – what if they decide to kill me too?*

Bile rose in my throat. The shock of its taste abruptly brought me into the present. I shifted on the box, became aware of the frozen blocks that were my feet. How long had I been sitting there? It might have been minutes or hours. I couldn't see the face of my watch. How much longer could I safely stay? And if I left – where would I go? Who could I talk to? James? Ha.

I thought of my father with sudden longing. If I were to tell him all this, what would he say? Would he come with me to the police?

My father... I swallowed. We'd just had that talk, and he'd advised me to close my eyes, to take the scholarship and ignore my feelings about Patrick Leyden. But I hadn't known any of this stuff then, and at least I could be sure that my father wouldn't mean me any harm. That he was a man of integrity.

But not of courage, or initiative. And he might not believe me either.

I put my hands up to my face. I couldn't think what to do. Turn myself in to Ms Wiles? Tell her I was crazy, that I believed I was crazy? Maybe that would be safest – I didn't want to die. I didn't want to take even the smallest risk. But if Daniel had been murdered – if Unity was the front for a drug distribution ring, now planning to expand into middle schools – utter evil, going after the younger kids...

Who knew what Ms Wiles had already been up to? People might be looking for me – scouring the campus and Lattimore.

I needed to think. Oh, God. I needed just a little more time and space and then surely, surely, I'd be able to figure out something to do.

It was then that I remembered Andy Jankowski. Andy, the only person on campus who could not possibly be involved in – whatever this was. Andy, who lived practically next door, above the garage.

29

I could hear no activity in the cottage any more, so possibly Ms Wiles had left. But it didn't really matter, from its previous life as a sunporch, the fake studio had its own door to the outside. I peeked round it cautiously and then slipped out into the calm darkness. It was the work of a moment to cross to the big white garage above which Andy Jankowski had his apartment. The windows on the second floor were dark, however. I lingered in the shadow of the building. What time was it? Could I wake Andy if he was there but asleep? How? Would loud knocking cause too much of a racket? There were other faculty apartments nearby – and people might be looking for me.

I stood helplessly, unable to move or make another decision.

And then, like a miracle, above my head a light went on. I stepped away from the side of the garage and looked up and, after a minute or two, a shade went up and Andy's face appeared at the window. He looked right out at me. I thought about lifting my hand to wave, but I didn't. It felt too heavy. I just kept staring upwards.

More lights snapped on in the apartment, and then another

one appeared behind the downstairs door. The door opened and Andy came outside. He was fully dressed, but with unlaced boots and coatless. He was carrying his coat, however. He came up to me and put it round my shoulders, on top of mine. I looked up at him, but it was too dark to read his expression.

"Frances Leventhal," he said. He sounded puzzled, and a little alarmed.

"I'm sorry," I whispered. My temples were pounding. "I needed a place to go. I just needed..." I couldn't go on. A friend. A real one.

"I woke up," Andy said slowly. "You were at Ms Wiles's. She was going to help you."

"She didn't help me. I needed a place to go. Could I – please – could I come in? Just for a little while." I could hear the desperation in my voice. I wondered if Andy would recognise it. If it would mean anything to him.

He said simply: "Yes. Come in, Frances Leventhal."

"Thank you," I managed. But for some reason I still couldn't move. Then Andy reached out a hand, took mine in it carefully, gently, and led me up the stairs inside and into his apartment.

Andy was an awkward host. He ushered me to an old, well-scrubbed kitchen table, removed a cardboard box from the second chair so I could sit there, and sat down himself, looking across at me for a full minute in uncertain silence before suddenly leaping up and pouring me a glass of milk. James's favourite beverage. I felt my shoulders tighten. I sipped at the milk anyway while Andy drank his own glass with an expression almost of relief at having thought of something to do. He fidgeted in his chair. He shot me frowning, nervous glances. The room was warm. I slipped off Andy's coat, and my own.

There was a big clock on the wall. Eleven thirty, it said.

"She didn't help you?" Andy asked suddenly. "That Ms Wiles?" The huge wrinkle across his forehead was deep.

I shook my head. I couldn't look at Andy, so I looked around the apartment.

It was a single, large room, with the irregular eaves and sloped ceiling of a space that had been created as an afterthought in an attic area. The walls were a bright, clean white and bare of pictures, plain horizontal blinds hung over the windows. Andy's single bed stood in the far corner against the wall. The living room area was defined by an old brown sofa, a green rug remnant, and a large television. In the kitchen nook, where I now sat, there was a sink and a stove, but no real oven, only a microwave.

Everything seemed extremely clean, and in perfect order. But the place was also very cluttered; there were piles of what looked like opened envelopes and catalogues on the floor and on most surfaces, and stacks of pristine cardboard boxes wherever they would fit. On the sides of some of them I could see original labelling: *Bounty paper towels, 16 count. Windex, 20 count.* All the stacks were in perfect alignment.

Even if Unity had had real work. Andy was too good for them.

Having examined the room, I studied the worn white spots on the kitchen table. It looked like it had been rescued from its tenth stay at the Salvation Army. There was something comforting about that, I thought. It was homely, and still useful.

Finally I could look at Andy. He was looking back at me quietly. He said, "She should have helped you."

I nodded. I still couldn't speak. I wanted to thank him for taking me in. I wondered if I could find the words to ask if I could sleep on his sofa. If I could just stay for the remainder of the night while I figured out what to do. I opened my mouth to try to get those things out. But instead I blurted, urgently: "Please can I use your bathroom?"

"Yes," Andy said. "It's that door over there, Frances Leventhal."

I felt panic nearly overcome me the moment I was alone in the tiny bathroom. Tears ran down my face. I turned on the cold water and bathed my cheeks and eyes for long minutes. Then, slowly, I raised my gaze to the mirror above the sink and looked at myself.

That blotchy face. The frozen expression.

That delicate yet sturdy-looking girl with the bushy hair and the Asian eyes.

Me. No. I still felt no kinship with her, but she was in trouble; she didn't know what to do. She didn't belong here, or anywhere. I pitied her. I feared for her.

I closed my eyes. I breathed. I splashed more water on the face that felt so disconnected from my inner self.

Finally I came out to find Andy pacing. He glanced at the door and my heart sank. Was he planning to escort me back to the dorm? Would he turn me in? Or maybe he'd done that already; my eyes flitted round the apartment until they found the telephone. Andy was, after all, a member of the school staff. It was probably his responsibility to turn me in.

"Did you call somebody about me?"

Andy stared. "Call?"

I faced him. "Please don't! Please don't turn me in, Andy. I just want – I just – please, Andy, please be my friend. I need help – I need..." I stopped talking. I looked down. I couldn't look at Andy. I hated myself. He was retarded. He had ten million problems of his own every day, I was sure. How dared I come to him? What was wrong with me? I was scaring him, I knew it. I had to stop, had to apologise, had to leave – right now, before I did any more damage to this nice man who was already the best friend he could be.

"I need someone," I said frantically again, instead. "I need a friend." I couldn't help it, I couldn't help saying it. The words just came out. Wrong place, wrong time, wrong person. Wrong me.

There was just silence.

I managed not to say anything else. I found my way to the sofa. I sat. I couldn't look at anything but my own forearms clutched to my stomach. Selfish, cowardly, stupid, weak, thoughtless, needy. Ugly Frances—

"Only Debbie ever asked me that before," Andy said. "Only Debbie is my friend." His voice wasn't angry or upset. There was something else in it. Something I couldn't quite identify, but even so, the vicious lecture in my head paused in its headlong pace and then... stopped. This was clearly important to Andy. This mattered.

I found the strength, the space in myself, to look up. Debbie. That was the woman who used to work in the cafeteria. I was suddenly sure of it. I thought Andy had mentioned her once before too. I said, "Tell me about Debbie."

Andy sat down across from me. His voice was slow and sad. "Debbie Angelakis. She needs help too."

Astonishingly, I felt a pang of jealousy for this Debbie, who was Andy's friend already. I swallowed it. "What kind of help?"

Andy leaned forward. "Debbie needs everything," he said simply. "But I don't know where she is now."

I was just feeling my way blindly here. "You don't know where she is?"

Andy nodded. "I sent letters to them at the hospital. Three times. I told them I could take care of her. I have a job and an apartment. The dean's secretary typed the letters for me on her computer so that they would look good. But no one answered. And now I don't know where Debbie is. I send letters to *her* too, but for a whole month the letters have been coming back. Return to sender. The dean called the hospital, and he says she isn't there any more, and no one knows where she is, and there's nothing anyone can do."

I stared at Andy. I wasn't sure what had shocked me more: what he'd said – the terrors it so matter-of-factly implied – or the glimpse it gave me of Andy's life, bigger, more complicated, more real, somehow, than I'd ever dreamed.

"I hope Debbie's not dead," Andy said starkly.

I was horrified. "But if she was OK a few weeks ago, then she can't possibly be—"

"She could so be dead." Never had I seen such naked fear – or helpless rage – in anyone's face. "They just put her on the street. That's what they do to people. And things happen. Things happen,

Frances Leventhal, and nobody cares. Even if she's not dead, she's out there somewhere. Alone. With no money or home. I want to go look for her. I would look on every street in Boston." He turned away suddenly. "But I have to wait for winter vacation."

"Oh," I said. "Oh. I'm so sorry." And I was. I didn't know what to do, or how to help. I blinked hard.

Silence then. But tentatively, warily, I looked up and so did Andy. "You really want me to be your friend?" Andy asked.

I nodded. Then I said, aloud, "Yes. And I want to be yours. I'm – I don't have much practice, but I think I could be a good friend, Andy."

He watched me. I realised I was holding my breath. I was filled with a kind of longing. It wasn't unlike the way I'd felt when I'd realised I was in love with James Droussian, and yet, at the same time, it was completely different.

Then Andy said, "I'll help you now, Frances Leventhal. We will try to be friends."

We reached out simultaneously. We clasped hands and shook, formally. Then, awkwardly, our hands fell apart.

"What do you need right now?" Andy added attentively. "What can I do?"

He's great, I realised. This man is great.

"What can I do?" said Andy again.

Whatever was happening with Unity, there was *still* only one thing I – we – could possibly do. Even though it might not necessarily help, I knew that we should simply go right away and tell the police what I knew, or thought I knew.

Right then, Andy's telephone rang loudly.

30

Every muscle in my body tightened. "Don't answer it," I said.

"OK," Andy said affably. We listened while the phone rang. Six, seven, eight times. Only then did I realise that Andy must not have any kind of answering machine or voice mail service. I bit my lip. Thirteen, fourteen... there were twenty insistent shrills before the ringing ceased.

I felt like there was a stone in my windpipe. I tried to swallow. It might have been Andy's friend Debbie, urgently trying to reach him. Or somebody else; who knew who? This was Andy's apartment, Andy's life. I had no right to assume the call was about me. No right to tell Andy what to do or not do in his own home.

I blurted: "I'm sorry. I was afraid it was Ms Wiles, looking for me."

Andy nodded, as if I'd had every right to tell him what to do. "She wouldn't help you before," he said.

I managed to take a deep breath. Later I would try to think of a way to help Andy find Debbie. Somehow I knew I had to do that. If I was his friend.

But now – I wasn't imagining things about Unity. This was urgent also. Andy wouldn't be able to help as much as Ms Wiles – the Ms Wiles of my imagination – could have. If she had existed. If she had really been my friend.

But Andy was the one who was here.

"Like I said before, I need your help," I said.

Andy nodded patiently. "Yes?"

How much did Andy need to know? How much would he understand? Carefully I said, "The stuff you told me about the fake work at the Unity food pantry? About the boxes that are always the same?"

"You believe me."

"Yes. I believe you." Then, all in a rush, I said, "Andy, would you be willing to come with me to the town police and tell them the same things?"

The deep wrinkle appeared again, straight across Andy's forehead. "The police," Andy said softly, reflectively.

"The Lattimore police," I confirmed.

I was completely tense again. It wasn't that I believed it would necessarily do much good. I knew exactly how credible Andy and I would look. A retarded man and a teenage girl – one who'd recently lost a brother and had just had some kind of tantrum or breakdown in the school cafeteria. And I was overwhelmingly aware of the power and influence wielded by Patrick Leyden. By The Pettengill School, which might even have been involved in ways I couldn't begin to imagine. I thought it very likely that a junior cop would listen to us and then show us the door.

But none of that could matter. When you think you have

knowledge of criminal activities, you ought to go to the police. That is what you ought to do. And... hope.

And – I thought of my mother in her Buddhist monastery – pray.

"OK," Andy said simply. He stood up. "Let's go."

I blinked up at him. Somehow I hadn't expected that we'd go immediately.

"You'll tell them about the boxes and about the fake work at Unity," I said again to Andy. "And I'll tell them what I know. That's all we have to do."

"I understand," said Andy.

"Wait," I said. I bit my lip. Maybe I was being ridiculous, but I found myself imagining Ms Wiles, and all kinds of Unity associates – Saskia, George de Witt, other teachers, maybe, possibly even James – discreetly combing the campus for me at this very moment. Untimely death – drug overdose – a faked suicide... *another* faked suicide...

A wave of pain for Daniel threatened to crash down on me, to drown me. I fought it – now was not the time...

Then, like a life preserver, an idea came to me. I grabbed at it frantically. "Wait!" I said again to Andy. "I think – I'm not sure, but I think that my dad might come with us. If I asked him. I could call him from here." I could trust my father; he wasn't perfect, but I could trust him. "He could come and get us in the car."

"OK," said Andy. "Call him." He sat down again.

A minute passed.

I looked at the telephone. I didn't move.

Another minute passed.

"Frances Leventhal," said Andy gently. "Are you scared?"

I shut my eyes. Then I opened them again and looked at Andy's kind, guileless face. I moved my head up and down.

"They killed your brother," Andy said.

For a moment I couldn't think a single coherent thought. How did Andy know about Daniel? Had he seen—? Did he have real facts he could tell the police? Had Andy all along been sitting on information—?

I managed to stutter, "How – how do you know that?"

"You said so," Andy answered. "Tonight, when we were walking home. Before I took you to Ms Wiles's apartment."

I had no memory of that at all. "I guess I forgot I said it."

"You didn't really notice me," Andy said, as if it didn't matter. "You were sort of talking to yourself."

I took in a shallow breath. "Oh."

"Do you really think that?" Andy asked. "About your brother."

I could almost feel the wave of pain as it towered before me, above me. It would engulf me if I let it – if I let myself know and feel everything at once. I could not. Not now.

"Yes," I said quietly. I looked down at my hands. "I really think that."

Andy nodded. "Then we have to go to the police," he said matter-of-factly.

I said, "I know." I stood up then, and so did Andy.

"I'll call my father," I said, though I didn't know what I would say to him, how I could formulate the words. I grasped the memory of my last conversation with him, of that fragile connection we'd forged. Then, with a sweaty palm, I reached for the phone and dialled.

It rang once, and then I was diverted to voice mail. I hung up hastily. I wondered who my father, or Bubbe, was talking to at – I finally looked at my watch – 12:45 a.m.

Then, on impulse, I moved to Andy's window and looked out on the Pettengill campus.

I felt Andy come up next to me. "It's snowing!" he said delightedly.

It was true, although it wasn't what I'd been staring at. Thick soft flakes were falling softly, beautifully, gently, turning the campus into a postcard – almost – of a New England night.

But the campus at this hour should have been much darker than it was. Instead the buildings that formed the main dormitory quad were all awake, alive. Light burned in nearly every window.

"What's going on?" Andy asked. "Why is everybody up?"

I wondered: were they looking for me? "I don't know."

"Should we go find out?"

I looked down at my hands. Then I said abruptly, "No. Let's just walk over to the police. Let's do it now."

Andy said, "OK." He fetched our coats.

"But – Andy?"

"Yes?"

I paused, trying to think clearly. With people up and about, it would be even more difficult to cross the campus unseen.

"I'm afraid people might be watching out for us. For me.

People that might not want us to go to the police. So we'll have to, well, sneak there. Secretly. Quietly. I know a path through the woods, away from the main road. So, um, can you sneak?"

"Yes," said Andy with dignity. "I can sneak." He had his coat on and buttoned. He handed me mine.

I put it on and fastened it. I exhaled. "OK," I said. I started towards Andy's door.

"Frances Leventhal?"

I turned. "Yes?"

Andy hadn't moved. He gestured towards one of his windows, on the opposite side of the room from the door. "If we're sneaking, maybe we should go out by the fire escape?"

I blinked at him.

"It goes to the other side of the garage, near the Dumpster. It's a better place to sneak away from," Andy explained. "I'll help you get down if you're scared."

"Thank you," I said. "Um. Good idea."

"Let's go, then," said Andy. "To the police." Solemnly he held out his hand, and I took it.

Out in the darkness, I could feel Andy beside me, and was overwhelmingly, gratefully conscious of how big and strong he was. And the falling snow lent a quiet, peaceful quality to the night.

"Let's take the maintenance road," Andy whispered. "Is the path you meant the one near the science centre?"

I whispered back, "Yes. We'll have to check before we use it – make sure nobody's there." In the snow, it was hard to believe that our mission was at all urgent. I thought of Ms Wiles's patent disbelief. If her studio hadn't been empty... But maybe, anyway, I was a fool. Maybe I was wrong... stupid.

As we walked, however, I felt the wires of tension tighten again round my spine. Now that we were outside, I could see that many other buildings were also lit up. The administrative building. Faculty apartments. In the distance, through the snow, I could see several dark figures scurrying along the campus paths.

What was going on? Would everybody really be up if they were just looking for a missing student, one who'd been gone only a few hours?

Maybe. Maybe, but—

The night that Daniel had been discovered – oh, God, it was only a month ago – the campus had also stayed awake. Just like this.

What had happened here in the last few hours?

The cold night air hurt my lungs. Beside Andy, I marched on. I told myself that Andy and I were just two more dark figures on the campus; if I couldn't recognise those other figures, then they couldn't recognise us. And no matter what was happening on campus, the best, the safest, the smartest thing for us to do right now was exactly what we were doing. Go to the police. Once we were there, we'd find out what was going on at Pettengill.

Without thinking, I reached out and grasped Andy's gloved hand with my own mittened one. He squeezed back, and I felt comforted. Accompanied. We swung our arms a bit as we walked together, and I remembered being little with Daniel.

We reached the maintenance road and angled to the left.

Slipped behind the science centre. There was the path, lightly covered with fresh snow.

And there, alone, leaning against a tree and looking directly towards us, was a shadowy figure that somehow I recognised instantly – not just with my eyes, but with my very skin. And in that moment I understood that I had come this way on purpose, knowing that he knew I used this path. Aware, in a way I can't explain, that if my "disappearance" were indeed some part of the commotion on campus, and if people really were looking for me, then he – James – would think to come here.

31

I stopped walking. I waited, strangely calm, as James pushed himself away from the tree and began to move through the falling snow towards Andy and me. As he approached, a spiral of disjointed images, aural memories, and emotions flashed through me.

The figures scurrying frantically across the Pettengill campus in the snow-muted glare of the dorm and campus lighting, just a few minutes ago. George de Witt, sitting with me in the cafeteria, saying that odd, out-of-place thing: *You're OK just how you are, Frances.* The traitorous warmth of Ms Wiles's cottage. Saskia, pushing me, yet understanding my paintings. My brother, Daniel, standing beside me in the old Leventhal shoe factory. The systematic, efficient way Andy had chopped the ice on the steps of the science centre. The feel of the crumpled paper cup in my hand, the smell of the alcohol in the punchbowl behind me at the freshman dance two years ago, when I'd glimpsed Saskia's lovely, confident face over Daniel's shoulder. In some way that I couldn't explain, but only feel, all of these moments had helped to bring me to this one.

Andy had stopped beside me. "That's James Droussian," he whispered loudly. "I don't think we can sneak past him now."

"No," I whispered back. "But it's OK. I think. He's – he's..." I didn't know how to continue.

Then James stood directly in front of us. "Hey," he said. "There you are."

"Hey," I said uncertainly. The disjointed feelings, images, had not gone away. I looked at James, before me in the gentle winter dark, and I also saw him as he'd been, not so long ago, in my grandmother's living room, as we sat shivah for Daniel. He'd been holding a glass of milk. He'd taken cookies from me as his eyes said to me: *You. You.*

My love, the drug dealer. My love, who didn't love me. Why didn't he scare me now? Why wasn't I frightened? For all I knew, James was involved with Unity. *Don't create opportunities for violence. Because if you do, violence will occur.* And there was the mysterious man he'd been with in the dark, in this very place. I'd never had an explanation.

I felt almost as if I'd taken some drug. A hallucinogenic, maybe, would feel this way. Everything seemed to be happening very slowly. I glanced down at James's hands. It was dark, yes, but I thought vaguely that I'd be able to tell if James was carrying, say, a gun. A rock. A hypodermic. I'd have a little bit of warning if Andy and I were going to die here.

But James's hands hung empty, ungloved, by his sides. And even in my reverie I was aware that I remained unafraid. Stubbornly, I believed that James meant no harm to me. That he would, in fact, always be kind to me. I kept my eyes on his empty hands and knew it. I knew it in every cell of my body.

Why did that make me feel so sad? So – defeated and empty?

James said steadily: "You're OK, Frances?"

I nodded. Everything had changed in a minute, in this minute, but I didn't understand why, or what, or, indeed, anything at all. I managed to look up at James's face, and was glad that it – and probably my face as well – was only a shadow in the dark. "Andy has been taking care of me," I said, and only when the words were out did I realise how true they were. I swallowed.

"We're going to the police," Andy said a little aggressively. "We have things to tell them."

James's head swivelled towards Andy, and after a second he nodded respectfully. "Not a bad idea. It's not really necessary now, but I'll walk you there if you want." He was looking back at me. *You, Frances. You.* "People were worried about you, Frances," he said quietly. "I was worried. I'm glad you're all right. Listen, I need to tell you some stuff. But the first thing is that you can stop – well, um, stop worrying. Things are going to be all right now."

I felt my head move in what could have been a nod, or a shake. What had James just said? It didn't seem to matter.

James was hatless. I saw how the lucky snow kissed his dark hair. I didn't have to see his face clearly to feel his continued focus on me.

Lie or not, I wanted to feel it. *You. You.*

Me. Me, standing before my grandmother as she waved her hand disparagingly beside my blossoming body. Me, reading about my father's invented oracle, who offered death in exchange for knowledge. Me, longing for the brother who didn't want my company, for the mother who wanted enlightenment, not me.

Me, full of ferocious, suppressed hate. Me, stomping on the snow in this very spot. Me, throwing my plate in the cafeteria. The delight of hearing it smash... of letting go. The fierce necessity to rein in again after that...

Things are going to be all right now, James had said. He was looking at me. He wanted me to say something. And I longed to believe him, but I knew he didn't possess the power to make things right.

Still—

"Things," I repeated cautiously, "are going to be all right?"

"Yes—" James began, but Andy interrupted.

"Why isn't it necessary to go to the police? I have something to tell them. You don't know what it is. Only Frances Leventhal knows."

I found myself nodding automatically.

"Andy," said James carefully. "Frances. Listen."

Me. Me, in the art studio, thinly applying the black acrylic that covered the paintings in my dorm room. Me, staring at the black fabric that covered my mirror.

"I'm afraid this is a little melodramatic," James said. "But it can't be helped." He opened his coat and reached for the inside breast pocket, and for a wild second I thought I'd been wrong after all, that he was reaching for a gun, a weapon, something.

My pulse pounded like hail on a roof.

Then the moment was over, and I was fully myself, standing in the woods with Andy and James. The snow fell gently around us, and James pulled out a little leather wallet. And then, just before he opened it – casually, routinely, and with one hand, just like in the movies – I knew what it was. What it had to be.

"Special Agent James Diefenbacher," said James quietly. He held up the wallet, or case, or whatever it was. It held a badge. "FBI."

"Oh," I said. After a numb second or two I took the badge from James's proffering hand. I examined it as best I could. I showed it to Andy, who fingered it carefully as well. We looked back up at James.

Special Agent James Diefenbacher.

"Wow," said Andy happily. "Federal Bureau of Investigation. You're a cop."

"Sort of," said James Diefenbacher. "Yes."

I looked at him and I saw what I had seen before, in the wee hours on a night not unlike this one, in this same spot. James talking with a man. Two men, together.

I had known. I could have known.

I hadn't wanted to see what was really there.

"FBI," I said.

James nodded. "There's been an investigation under way at Pettengill for some time, Frances. But it's ending now, and everything is going to be OK."

Andy said with excitement: "If you're a cop, I can tell *you* about the boxes."

"Boxes?" asked James.

"Boxes," said Andy firmly. "Fake work at the Unity food pantry."

James looked at Andy in silence. Then his gaze shifted to me. And then he nodded. "Unity. Yes. Frances, I can tell you – and Andy – not everything, but a lot. Not now, not tonight, but soon. For now, just know that everything is going to be OK."

Another lie. Mingled sadness and shame pressed at my throat. I wondered how old James Diefenbacher was. Ten years older than me? Twelve? It didn't matter. It was an impassable gulf. One of many. I had been a delusional fool. And James knew what I felt. Of course he knew. It was one reason why he was being so kind.

"Unity," I said steadily. "They're a front for a drug ring?" The snow fell lightly, gently. I felt it on my face.

"Yes," said James Diefenbacher. His mouth twisted. "Congratulations. You figured that out quickly."

I had to ask. "My brother?" I said. "He didn't kill himself, did he?"

James's shoulders moved uneasily. After a moment: "Frances—"

"Please."

Another moment. Then: "No. We think not."

"They killed him?" My throat was full, I could barely get the words out. Dimly I felt Andy take my hand and squeeze it.

"Frances. You'll find out – perhaps not everything, but most of your questions will be answered soon. Please wait. The investigation is over as of tonight. Tomorrow, maybe, I can talk to you. Let me walk you both somewhere that you can rest. To the police, if you'd still like. Or home to your father." He made a gesture, moved as if to herd Andy and me on to the path.

All at once I was filled with strength. Or stubbornness, which passed for the same thing.

"Why is your investigation over as of tonight?" I asked. "What's happened? What did you do?" Involuntarily I glanced over my shoulder, back towards the unquiet campus. "What's happening at Pettengill right now? Why all the lights? Is this related to – to–" I stopped. I couldn't think how to word my question. "To Unity?" I said finally.

Another silent moment. Then James Diefenbacher, Special Agent, shrugged. "Yes," he said. "It's actually almost funny. We – our team – was scooped, in a way. We spent all this time looking fruitlessly for an informant, and all the time someone inside Unity was collecting, without us, all the evidence any prosecutor could ever want. Tape recordings, bank account statements, client lists, evidence samples. Everything meticulously documented. Labelled. Dated."

My mouth had gone dry. "Who?" I whispered. "Who got all that?"

"Saskia Sweeney," said James Diefenbacher. "She's blown this whole thing wide open."

And as I gaped at him, he added: "Yeah, I know. It's made us–" He paused and looked straight into my eyes before continuing. "That is, my partner, Yvette, and me – look and feel extremely stupid."

Yvette? I thought. *My partner, Yvette?*

My brain stopped functioning entirely. It was all I could do to hear the words James Diefenbacher was saying.

"You see, we'd written Saskia off as a possible informant. In fact, we'd written off finding any inside informant at all. Leyden was just too good at picking people that he could trust. Unity was as tight and impenetrable as a fortress.

"Our last hope – and it was a feeble one, with Yvette and me in disagreement on how or if we should do it – was actually you, Frances.

"We thought maybe you could be manipulated into joining Unity, and that maybe you would succeed in getting evidence we could use."

32

At the start of February school break, Special Agents Diefenbacher and Sorensen drove me to Boston to visit Saskia, who was being kept in "protective custody". Sorensen – I tried very hard to think of her by that name, to separate her from the Ms Wiles by whom I still felt used, betrayed – said that Saskia had asked specifically, urgently, if I could visit her.

A living mass of nerve endings, I sat in the back seat of the Ford Taurus. But the nerves were nothing new. I had been in this state for all of the long days since the Unity scandal had exploded at Pettengill and in the media. Still, it didn't help that my stomach was now roiling with the motion of the car, and that I had started menstruating last night. Grimly, I had already taken aspirin. I already knew that this was going to be one of my painful periods.

I was anxious about seeing Saskia. I both did and didn't want to hear whatever it was that she had to say to me. I both did and didn't want to say and ask the things that were burning in my throat, my chest. And it went without saying that I had very mixed feelings about being confined in a car for hours, going and coming, with Sorensen and Diefenbacher.

But I also knew I couldn't have stayed at Pettengill today, hanging out with Andy, going over our growing plans for looking for his friend Debbie. Today I had to do this.

Daniel's voice came suddenly into my head, sounding just as sarcastic as ever. *If there is no wound on one's hand, one can handle poison.* I closed my eyes tightly for a moment and thought about that. What did it mean? Had Daniel thought he could safely handle poison? Was that why he'd made the choices he had? But he had turned out to be wounded... unsafe...

I felt myself shudder. My brother. My brother...

All the things I'd learned about Daniel – and the remaining, terrible question: How *exactly* had he died? – seemed to float in my mind where they could be seen but not touched. I wasn't sure if I had the strength to reach out towards them. To know them. And yet that was what I was going to do. Today. Now.

Could I handle poison? I hope so. I felt... surrounded by it. And yet I was out of places to hide. I was past, really, wanting to hide. I was resigned.

The car was warm. I wriggled out of my coat and absently stroked the sleeve of my new cashmere cardigan. It made me feel just a little bit comforted.

The sweater had arrived yesterday in a box from Nordstrom, a mysterious catalogue order from my father. I doubted he could afford it and I had almost sent it back. But staring at it, touching it, I had been filled with unexpected longing. It was pure white, and somehow I'd known it would look good on that mirrored girl. On – on me.

I'd told myself that wearing the new sweater would help me

face Saskia. But I knew, as I lifted it gently, tentatively, to my cheek – it was so soft! – that that was not why I was keeping it.

I was keeping it because it was so pretty. I was keeping it because I wanted to feel it against my skin. I was keeping it because, as I held it, and stroked it, I *wanted* it – so much, I could have cried. Or screamed.

I couldn't bear to analyse it. I just – kept the sweater.

No one in the car said anything. Sorensen was driving. She had tuned the radio to a classic rock station on which Eric Clapton was half declaring, half praying: "No more bad love". Diefenbacher crooned along. His voice was so nearly inaudible that I wondered if he even realised I could hear him.

I looked away from the back of his head and sat quietly with that other pain that never went completely away.

He had offered me the front seat for this trip, but I'd refused. Sitting in the back emphasised that Sorensen and Diefenbacher were the adults. Diefenbacher was, I now knew, eleven years older than me. He was even wearing a suit and tie. To him I was just too young to think of romantically. Sexually. And to him my recent personal revelation, deep in the dark of another sleepless night, was irrelevant.

Whatever else I might or might not be, I was not a child. I had had the body of a woman for seven years now. *Seven* years.

A confirming cramp bit into my abdomen. It was almost like an old friend. I pressed my forearm against my stomach and looked out the window at the trees beside Interstate 93.

I closed my eyes and concentrated on remembering the facts about this whole mess, as I had learned them over the last days, not only from the media, but from talking to Diefenbacher and Sorensen, over coffee, yesterday.

They had been good to me yesterday, Diefenbacher and Sorensen. Well, they had tried. In the abandoned cafeteria at Pettengill they had answered all of my questions. Or, at least they had answered the ones I was able to ask. We all knew, I think, that some things – some personal things – could never be asked, or answered, or even acknowledged.

I didn't want to know if Diefenbacher had realised how I felt about James Droussian. I didn't want to know if Sorensen had told him her thoughts about that.

I had actually been fascinated by the coverage of the scandal in the media. Somehow the reporters and TV people had largely been kept away from Pettengill itself, so I felt safely distanced as I – along with everyone else on campus – kept up with the latest public information. CNN and the *Boston Globe* and *Dateline* seemed to be following along in my mental footsteps. It was satisfying in a twisted kind of way, to watch the story unfold.

FBI AND SEC HOLD JOINT PRESS CONFERENCE

COGNITIVE REACH STOCK CRASHES IN REVELATIONS ABOUT INITIAL VENTURE CAPITAL FINANCING

PRESIDENT OF INTERNET FIRM ARRESTED

PREP SCHOOL LEADERS JOIN TOGETHER TO REASSURE PARENTS, STUDENTS

IS YOUR TEEN DEALING DRUGS? TEN WARNING SIGNS FOR PARENTS

The stories had dominated the business and education news for days, but were beginning to fade now – "At least," Sorensen had said yesterday in the cafeteria, "until the legal stuff gets fully under way."

"Uh-huh," I'd replied, marvelling again that this unfamiliar woman was – had been – my Ms Wiles. I did not look directly at James – at Diefenbacher – but I could see him anyway, in the periphery of my vision.

"Did you read this yet, Frances"? Sorensen asked, pushing a current news magazine across the table and pointing to a headline. HOW IT BEGAN: LEYDEN AND FRIENDS FORM UNHOLY ALLIANCE. "It's the best synopsis of the business end that I've seen so far."

I had in fact read the article that morning, but I bent over it anyway, scanning it again. For all I'd wanted this meeting with both of them, wanted my questions answered, now I was not quite ready.

Patrick Leyden started Unity Service as a senior at the exclusive Pettengill preparatory school, after two years running his own small drug distribution operation. Even at eighteen he had organisational genius, and he worked out a plan to recruit younger students for the charity, with a trusted few in each class understanding and operating the real business. Throughout his college years, he stayed involved, becoming the major force behind expanding the drug ring to other prep schools and turning it into a mostly wholesale business.

As the associated students graduated and became

alumni, they stayed involved, helping with the expansion. A handful of school faculty members and one administrator were also recruited as permanent partners. Leyden proved uncannily good at determining who was vulnerable to long-term involvement as a so-called "salaried adviser". (See graph on teacher salaries.)

Using the "food pantry" work as cover, the organisation was able to buy drugs in large quantities and redistribute them efficiently.

In addition the charity proved to be an excellent way to launder money. Cash poured in and was labelled as charitable contributions. This proved attractive to purchasers: who wouldn't want to buy their cocaine on a tax-deductible basis?

Leyden then used his profits from the false charity to provide the initial venture capital funding for his legitimate business – the Internet start-up Cognitive Reach.

Ironically, this eventually proved to be Leyden's downfall. Two years ago, in the period before the first offering of Cognitive Reach stock to the public, an analyst for the Securities and Exchange Commission became curious during a routine check into the venture capital funding of the company.

Since start-up investing at that level is quite risky, it is usually only done by very experienced and wealthy individuals, or family members. But Leyden's money had all come from a group of very young investors, none of whom had ever invested in a start-up before, and none of whom had any obvious sources for the money themselves.

The SEC analyst contacted the FBI's financial and computer-related crime divisions, who eventually contacted the drugs and interstate racketeering division. A complex investigation with undercover elements began...

I could feel both Diefenbacher and Sorensen watching me while I read the article. I took my time. Finally I looked up.

"You figured out a lot of this stuff yourself," said Diefenbacher.

I shrugged, even though inwardly I was warmed by the approval I saw in his face. "Well," I said. I fidgeted, smoothing one hand over the magazine. I took a deep breath then, and began my questions. "What part of the FBI do you two work for?"

"RICO," said Diefenbacher. "That's, uh – racketeering. Organised crime."

"I'm in finance," said Sorensen. When I stared at her, surprised again, she added – did I imagine a bit defensively? – "Well, it's *interesting*. And art history was my minor at college, not my major."

I didn't know her, I reminded myself. I didn't know who she was at all. I asked, "When did you – the FBI – begin focusing on Unity and Pettengill?"

"Almost right away after the SEC contacted us," Diefenbacher said. "It wasn't difficult to figure out that Pettengill was the common link between the initial Cognitive Reach investors and Leyden. Leyden's involvement with Unity was public knowledge. And then a detailed audit of Unity's books turned up some other financial peculiarities." He seemed to understand that I just wanted him to keep talking. "We, uh, took a look round the buildings – the Unity food pantry, and that of similar pantries at some other prep schools – and soon we knew what was going on. We could have stopped the whole thing a year ago."

I sat up straighter. A year ago my brother was still alive. "Why *didn't* you stop it a year ago?"

"Because we had to have Leyden!" Sorensen said, leaning forward. "Leyden himself, not the students. We needed direct evidence of Leyden's involvement, and the only way to get it was an undercover investigation. And imagine – we had to stand idly by last year and watch Leyden get that Presidential Freedom Award. Orders. It was unbelievable."

Sorensen had gone undercover at Pettengill first, using her undergraduate minor in art history and some falsified teaching credentials to get the art teacher job.

"Yvette worked hard to try to get inside Unity herself," Diefenbacher said. "But all they let her do was attend charitable meetings and pack clothing once a month. And her attempts to get close to the students and faculty members who seemed to be on the inside were just as futile. So I enrolled as a post-grad student at the beginning of last September and tried to establish myself as a shady character of the kind that Unity might like to recruit. And no one paid any attention at all."

I wondered about the ethics of an FBI agent actually dealing drugs, even as an undercover agent. I remembered James saying to me once that he wouldn't sell smack. Was that the line? It seemed arbitrary.

It made me feel queasy.

Diefenbacher had gone on. "That was another miscalculation on our part. We hadn't yet figured out that by now Leyden's student recruits were all on scholarship. That was another brilliant idea of Leyden's. The scholarships were created with the thought that the recipients would be good recruits for the real work. More easily seduced, more easily controlled."

Like Daniel, I thought. I said, "Was any of Unity's charity work legitimate?"

"Some, we think. The cash grants to families in need. The scholarships were real, as you know. And they did donate overflow clothing and shoes and so on to the Salvation Army. But they never did any real distribution of charitable goods themselves. Goods went round and round, as Andy Jankowski figured out. And *we* went round and round, trying to find an angle on Leyden."

"And then Daniel died," I said quite calmly.

"And then Daniel died," Diefenbacher confirmed. "And we noticed you. We realised that you could potentially get inside Unity. We thought they might need someone new, with Daniel gone."

I thought about being at that Unity meeting, with James declaring that I shouldn't do what Leyden wanted, while Ms Wiles said that I should. For a second I thought that under no circumstances did I want to hear Yvette Sorensen justify to me why Ms Wiles – my supposed friend! – had tried to influence me into joining Unity and, perhaps, becoming their informant. Why she'd been able to risk my emotional – and physical – welfare in that way. But I took a quick breath anyway and said, "So you two decided to play good cop-bad cop to try to manipulate me into joining."

There was a moment of silence. Then Diefenbacher said, "Not exactly." He was looking directly back at me. His eyes still said *You*, but I was ice. "Yvette and I disagreed about this. To me it felt too desperate, and I didn't think they'd trust you. But—" He cleared his throat. "But we were in agreement about *you*. We knew that if you did get in, if you discovered what was going on, you'd help us get Leyden. You'd do whatever you could."

Listening to his voice, I remembered sitting across a cafeteria table from him when he was James Droussian, on a day that had felt, to me, like spring.

"We knew you had integrity, Frances. We knew you were honest."

"Yes," said Sorensen. "There was never the slightest doubt about that." I wouldn't look at her. "It's in your work, Frances. It's in everything you do."

How strange to hear something good about yourself, and to believe it.

I put it aside.

"Anyway, it didn't work out the way you two planned," I said to my hands. "I talked to Andy and figured out a few things, and panicked. And I see now that if Saskia hadn't done what she did, I would have messed up everything. Or maybe even got killed, like my brother. And Leyden would have got away."

"Well, perhaps," said Sorensen dryly. "But don't worry about that. You didn't do any worse than we did. As you know."

More long, awkward silence had filled the cafeteria then. And into it, finally, I asked, "So. How did my brother die, exactly? How did he come to be killed?"

In my mind I could see Daniel in the lotus position, shaking his head. *No, no, no.*

Around me, that same silence. And then Sorensen said, "Saskia Sweeney has asked that she be the one to tell you about Daniel's death. If you agree, we can drive you up to Boston tomorrow to see her."

"Oh," I had said uncertainly. "Saskia."

I had a moment of all-too-familiar fear. I thought: what difference did it make exactly how Patrick Leyden had had Daniel killed? I knew Daniel had been involved with Unity, up to his neck in drug distribution and evil. Did I really want any more details? Did I need them? Did I want to hear what Saskia had to say?

No. I did not. But... but... I also *had* to.

I pushed the fear back.

"OK," I had said. "I'll talk to Saskia."

"We're here," said Diefenbacher now, as I clutched my stomach against another round of cramps. I looked up and discovered that we had parked in front of a large brick apartment building.

Saskia, I thought. Saskia is in there. I took a deep breath.

I got out of the car.

33

"Hello, Frances," said Saskia.

She was standing just beyond the apartment's small foyer, balancing somehow with legs crossed and one sock-clad foot on top of the other. She wore ancient jeans, the tails of a red flannel shirt hung over her hips. I stared in shock – she looked so sloppy! And yet somehow she looked comfortable, at ease in her skin, despite the situation. Despite everything.

Her gaze was fixed on me like a laser beam. Just behind her I could see a middle-aged uniformed woman sitting on a sofa and pecking away at a laptop computer. A cop.

"Hello," I said. My cramps clutched at me again but I tried not to react. Not in front of Saskia.

"We can talk in my room." Saskia jerked her head towards a hall to her left. Her hair was tucked behind her ears, and I could see the empty pinprick holes for her earrings. "OK, Maria?" Saskia's tone had gone slightly sarcastic. I followed her gaze to the policewoman on the sofa.

"Fine," said the policewoman calmly. I noticed that she was wearing a gun. "Leave the door ajar." I saw Saskia wince before her face smoothed out again into blandness.

The policewoman was looking at me now. "Did they say they'd be back to pick you up in two hours?"

"Yes." I wished it were fifteen minutes. From across the room I could feel Saskia's intensity.

I followed her into a small room with a daybed, a nightstand, and a desk on which a pile of familiar textbooks were stacked. The novel *Beloved* sat right on top, looking as untouched as my own copy. "They got a tutor for me," Saskia said, noticing where I was looking. "Like it matters." Somehow she had moved behind me, blocking my access to the door. "Have a seat," she said.

There should have been a chair in front of the desk, but there wasn't. Uneasily, I settled down on an end of the daybed. I tucked one leg beneath myself, keeping the other on the floor. But then I heard Bubbe's mocking voice in my head: *Ready to run?* I put both feet on the floor. I'd run if I wanted to. I placed one arm against my stomach so that I could press on it, when I needed to, in an unobtrusive way.

Saskia plunked herself down at the other end. Seated, our different heights ceased to matter and, although separated by three feet of mattress, we were eye to eye. As I looked at her, I thought with the old wonderment and resentment that she was still beautiful. She was still what I wished I were. And she was the one who had exposed Patrick Leyden. She was the one who had avenged Daniel. She was the heroine of the drama, while I had only walked on and bumbled around in the last act.

"Well," I said uneasily. "Are you OK? Are they treating you all right?"

Saskia shrugged. "Sure. I have a lawyer. They let my mum visit. Of course, there's the twenty-four-hour security – they think Patrick might try to have me killed – but I'm adjusting to that." At my expression, her lips twisted and she added, "Oh, don't worry about it. I know Patrick better than they do and believe me, it's the last thing on his mind. He's busy with his lawyers, writing cheques, trying to figure out an escape strategy."

Patrick, I thought. "If he's got smart lawyers and lots of money—"

"No," Saskia interrupted. Twin red spots appeared in the middle of her cheeks. "He's not getting out of this. Listen, I got bank statements and accurate money trails. I got tape recordings. I got drug bags with his fingerprints on them. I have a diary over the last six months that details every meeting, every conversation, every decision. I knew what I was doing. I have him tied up."

I knew that Diefenbacher and Sorensen thought the same thing. "Well, then," I began.

But Saskia wasn't finished. Words poured from her in a torrent. "Not only that, but he's going to be bankrupt soon, so he won't be able to afford a fleet of lawyers. Get this – it's so good I can't stand it. Patrick had just bought back a lot of his own stock. But of course Cognitive Reach's stock price went right into the toilet last week, and he lost fifty million dollars! The stock won't recover until the company dissociates itself from him, which of course they're doing fast. So Patrick is going to lose his beloved Cognitive Reach, Frances, along with all his credibility and stature and reputation. By the time the SEC and the IRS and his own lawyers are through with him, he'll be a pauper."

Her eyes gleamed with triumph – and something else. Pain?

"And you know what, Frances? I'm the one who did it. I'm the one who ruined him. Me, little Saskia. He knows it. And he'll know it even more as things get worse and worse for him. Until finally he's in jail, choking on it."

I was silent. I had never seen such hatred. What had caused it? Why did Saskia hate Leyden so much? It had to be about Daniel.

Watching Saskia, I was more than a little awed. I thought back to when she had promised to make my life miserable, and I remembered how I had countered her but inside had curled up with terror. I had been right to fear Saskia. If she had really wanted to make my life miserable, she could have.

She must not have wanted to, then. How could I ask her? I said carefully, "When you didn't want me to join Unity, I thought..."

"What? That I was being a hateful bitch?"

I nodded.

The red spots on Saskia's cheeks were fading back now into white. "And what do you think now?"

I stumbled. "Were you – were you trying to protect me?"

Her gaze shifted away from me, then back. "I had work to do. Maybe I just didn't want you getting in my way."

"Oh," I said. The silence elongated. Suddenly I had to press my forearm to my abdomen, hard.

Saskia asked clinically, "Cramps?"

"Uh-huh."

"I thought so. I get them too." She regarded me closely. "Maybe not so bad, though."

I had had to close my eyes for a few seconds. Finally the wave of pain passed. I looked up again. Saskia seemed... closer. She burst out, "Look, I'm not really sure, OK? I just – didn't want you involved."

"I wondered..." I gathered myself. "I wondered if it was because of Daniel. I wondered if maybe Daniel was protecting me too, all those times he was so horrible to me about Unity..."

I looked across into Saskia's face. I read an answer there: No.

But then she said, "Yes. Yes, exactly. I was doing what Daniel wanted. Unity was fine for him, and for me, but the last thing he wanted was his little sister involved in it. He went out of his way to alienate you. He wanted to make sure you'd never want to be where he was, doing what he was doing. What I was doing."

"You're lying," I said.

Her eyes dropped away from mine.

The world had tilted on its axis for me. I said after a moment, "I'm sorry, Saskia. I was jealous of you. Of you and Daniel both."

She shrugged. "I was jealous of *you*. For other reasons. You seemed so... OK on your own. You didn't need anybody. You just stayed yourself, and that saved you." Her mouth twisted, and she quoted, in perfect mimicry of Daniel doing his Buddha thing: "*Guard yourself like a frontier town.* That was what you always did."

I gaped at her.

And then softly she said: "Daniel treated me like dirt, you know."

Somehow I found my voice. "No..."

"Yes." And as I continued to stare, she added, "You are so naïve, Frances. I never understood how you could be that way. I still don't understand. You're not stupid. Just... blind. Oblivious."

"Daniel loved you," I said finally, uncertainly. "Didn't he?"

"Daniel loved only himself. And the thought of being rich."

We looked at each other.

Finally I asked: "Did you – didn't *you* love *him*?"

Saskia shrugged again. "At the beginning I did. When we were first at Pettengill. He made me feel less alone. When I was with him – having a boyfriend, you know – I felt more like I belonged." Then: "Frances, are you OK?"

"Yes," I said grimly, conscious that it wasn't just the cramps that had me in anguish. I was pressing against my stomach with both arms now. "This is... pretty normal for me. First day. You know." Finally I could look up again.

The conversation had not gone the way I had thought it would go. And there was something else. Something hidden, the way I'd hidden my own nightmares beneath black paint. I could feel it. I could feel it in the room with us. I said, "Saskia?"

She tilted her head to the side. "Yes?"

And my nerve, my courage, was right there with me, steady. Calm. I said, "I was told you wanted to talk to me about Daniel's death. That you would tell me how it happened."

"Yes," said Saskia. Had she paled even more? "That's true."

"OK," I said. I took a deep breath. "Then let's do it. Get it over with, Saskia. I can handle it. Tell me how Patrick Leyden killed Daniel."

She was too silent.

"Saskia?" I said.

She said, "Well, that's just it. Patrick Leyden didn't kill Daniel. Maybe he was ultimately responsible – my lawyer plans to say that, and that it was self-defence, in a way. But Leyden wasn't directly responsible."

Her eyes were twin pits of hell. "Frances. I killed Daniel."

34

"You're quiet," said Diefenbacher to me from the driver's seat.

"Uh-huh," I said. He and I had been in the car, alone, for five minutes only. It was odd. I realised now that on the drive up, I'd secretly longed to have Sorensen not be there. Despite everything, I'd wanted to be alone for a single, precious, even silent hour with James – with Diefenbacher. But now that I had got my wish for the drive back, I didn't care.

Diefenbacher had given me a note from Yvette, who was staying in Boston overnight. He had said that she wanted me to call her, that she wanted to talk to me. I had nodded and stuffed the note in my pocket, but I didn't think I could call her. I didn't think I'd want to talk to her ever again.

As we drove slowly through the evening rush-hour traffic, I watched out the window of the car. On the sidewalk in front of a brownstone, I saw a couple who seemed to be about my age; a tall boy with a shaved head – shaved so close he was really bald – had his arm round a girl with short, dyed-white hair. She was laughing up into his face and he was grinning down at her and, despite the difference in their heights, their steps matched perfectly as they walked, leaning into each other and battling the winter wind. In love, I thought, and abruptly had to blink hard.

When I could focus again, the car had moved on, leaving the couple behind. I realised that my cramps had subsided to dull, intermittent stabs and was grateful for that, at least. The car was warm. I stripped off my mittens and opened my coat.

A silent Diefenbacher was trying to work the car over to the highway. Right now, however, we had come to a standstill. Hoping masochistically for another glimpse of the happy young couple, I looked out at the bundled-up pedestrians, the dirty snow, the anxious cars. No couple, but in the Toyota next to us a man abruptly hurled his cell phone away and then looked directly at me and gave me the finger. Then he smashed down on his horn.

"Yeah, that'll help," James muttered. Despite the nasty traffic and his attention to it, I could feel that James's – Diefenbacher's – real awareness was of me. There was some small satisfaction in that. It was very small, however.

"Saskia told you?" James said, his eyes straight ahead. "About Daniel?" And then, when I didn't reply: "Frances?"

"Yes," I said. "She told me." I leaned my right elbow on the car's armrest and angled my body more sharply towards the window. The man in the Toyota was gripping his wheel with both hands. His eyes were closed. Suddenly I noticed that there was a toddler in a car seat in the back of his car. The child's mouth was open.

I could paint that, I thought. I could paint that man, in that car, with that baby. First I'd wash the entire canvas in dark red –

no, better, red with a greyish tint. Oils for this. Not acrylics.

"Are you OK?" James persisted.

"No," I said calmly. I'd use a thick brush, I thought. I'd make the baby all head. One big head bouncing in the back seat, while his father leaned with huge fisted hands on the wheel in the front. And white headlights all around. The light would be sharp needles attacking the car.

Saskia had deliberately injected Daniel, while he slept, with an overdose of heroin. She had watched, beside him, until he died.

"I wrote the note in advance," she told me. "I planned everything in advance. This was not an accident. It was murder, Frances. I made love to Daniel that night, and then I murdered him."

There was actually pride in her voice. Pride, and terror, and something I couldn't name. I looked at her and she looked back at me, and it had been as if we were trapped, doomed to stare and stare... my whole body had felt frozen...

"I want to help you," James said. He didn't look at me, and he sounded calm, but beneath the calm I thought I could hear a certain urgency, determination, in his voice. "Terrible things have happened, Frances. It might take you years to absorb them and come to terms with them. If you ever can."

I didn't reply.

"I know you loved your brother. I know what Saskia told you must have been a terrible shock. It was to me, and I knew things you didn't, and – well, of course, he wasn't my brother."

I said nothing.

"And I know that – that the bad things about Daniel – I know that, in a way, they don't matter. He was your brother... But if it would help you to talk... and I think it might... We were friends, Frances, you and I. Are friends. Aren't we?"

I didn't think so. I said softly, "I don't want to talk."

Some minutes passed. Then: "OK," said James.

The traffic finally began to move. The man in the Toyota turned off to the right. I closed my eyes. And I was back in the apartment building, in Saskia's tiny room, sitting across from her. Listening, listening, in a time-space vacuum that contained only us, face to face, staring into each other's eyes, each other's souls.

"It all happened quickly." Saskia's voice was flat, factual. "One morning Daniel found my tapes, all my accumulated evidence. He'd secretly made a copy of my room key. I walked in and found him sitting with my Walkman, listening to a tape. He'd torn my closet apart looking – he told me he'd suspected I was taping conversations.

"I tried to bluff. I told Daniel it was just insurance, leverage to use against Patrick if we needed to. That it was for both of us. He said he understood. But I watched his eyes as we pretended to believe each other, and I knew he'd tell Patrick. It was only a matter of time. Patrick was due at Pettengill the next day, and if he knew what I was doing—" She swallowed.

"Daniel didn't get it, Frances. Patrick Leyden was ruining both our lives, and he didn't see it. Daniel didn't see what he had become. He didn't see how bad – how – or he didn't care.

"We had both become monsters. I didn't understand at first,

I just liked having more money. I didn't see what I – what I...
And then one day I did see. Last September, when Patrick
started talking about middle schools. It was like waking up
from a dream – like a slap. Suddenly I understood: we might
be hurting – killing, destroying – thousands of people. And
Daniel – I remember he laughed and said—"

She stopped. I watched her fists clench.

"What?" I said. "Saskia? What did Daniel say?"

She wasn't looking at me now. I waited.

Then she seemed to gather herself. "It doesn't matter," she
said flatly.

"But Saskia—"

"No!" Saskia said sharply. Then, after a while she added,
still not looking at me: "Frances, you can't possibly understand
– I don't *want* you to understand – what it's like to suddenly
see how ugly you are. You, and the people you've chosen to be
with..."

My throat closed.

"Look, I thought I had to kill Daniel," Saskia said rapidly. "I
thought I had to. I had to get Patrick. I had sworn to myself
that I – and I don't know. I looked at Daniel and I knew it was
too late for him. Maybe I was crazy that day. Maybe I've been
crazy for months. Or years. But that day I only saw one way for
me to – to go on. It seemed to be a choice between one person
or thousands."

Suddenly she looked directly at me. "I still only see one
way," she said. "The way I took." She reached out then. She
reached out across the length of the bed and gripped both my

hands in hers. She gripped them tightly, tightly, and it hurt.

"It was easy, Frances," she whispered, and the words went right into me and lodged like shards of glass. I knew they would never come out. "Killing Daniel was actually very easy.

"And this is the thing. This is what I want you to know. It was him or me, Frances. It was. If I hadn't shut Daniel up, Patrick would never have been caught. That's important, right? Isn't it?"

I looked at her.

"Please," said Saskia to me. "Please, Frances, tell me you understand it's important."

She didn't say, "Tell me you forgive me." But I heard it. I heard it, and I saw it in her beautiful, beautiful face.

You don't know what it's like, she had said, *to suddenly understand how ugly you are.*

I didn't answer. I stared at her, and she stared at me. And my hands moved a little, in hers, and – almost against my will – gripped back.

I wanted to ask: why, Saskia? Why exactly do you hate Patrick Leyden so much? Is it just because of the thousands of kids that you think destroying him might have saved? Or is it something more... personal?

The difference in age between Saskia and Patrick Leyden was actually less than between me and James Droussian – Diefenbacher.

I wanted to ask. I wanted to ask because this too was one of the answers to why Daniel had died. I wanted to ask.

But I didn't.

I was not ready to know.

We had made it to the highway, where the traffic remained thick but did move. I wondered how long it would take to get back to Pettengill. I was supposed to have dinner in the cafeteria with Andy. I wondered if he'd mind if I cancelled. If I just went to bed.

Or maybe it would be better for me to keep busy. To take the bus to Boston tomorrow with Andy as planned, and visit the hospital, talk with the nurses and doctors and social workers who'd known Debbie there... yes. Yes. I'd do that. Yes, that was best. Andy was so excited, so hopeful. And perhaps – who knew? – maybe we would find Debbie. Find her, take her back on the bus with us, help her make a life. Keep her from dying. If I could be part of that, then maybe, maybe...

"Frances, I wish you'd say something," Diefenbacher – James – said quietly. "Anything."

I looked over at his profile. It was nearly full dark outside now. I wet my lips. I said, "OK. Tell me, Special Agent Diefenbacher. Do you like working for the FBI? How do you feel about all of – all of this? Good? Do you like working neck-deep in —" I groped for a word and, to my surprise, found it. "In evil?"

I heard Daniel's Buddha voice in my head suddenly, and for once it wasn't sarcastic. He was whispering. *A whole water pot will fill up from dripping drops of water. A fool fills himself with evil a little at a time.*

Perhaps that was what had happened.

"Aren't you afraid?" I said to James. I could hear in my voice that tears weren't far away, but I wouldn't let them come any closer. I said what I wanted to say. "Aren't you afraid you'll get infected? Or that, some day, you won't know the difference between – between—" I stopped then. I couldn't go on.

Oh, God. What had my brother thought he was doing? Who was he? What had he believed? And who – who was I?

I buried my face in my hands.

Then, in the darkness, James answered. Almost. He said: "I feel good about Patrick Leyden being in jail. Not to mention his ten best pals. I feel good about their probable futures." Another second, and then: "The world is not a pretty place, Frances. But I know where I stand in it. I do my best out there."

I looked up. I wasn't crying. "Fighting evil?" I said hoarsely. I wanted it to be sarcastic, but somehow it wasn't. It was just – sad.

A few seconds passed and then James said, "Yes. That was the idea. Doing what I can. I can't say I never have regrets, but I'm not sorry to be out there trying." I thought he was done, but then he added quietly: "Every one of us is needed."

I thought of how Daniel had said similar things originally. About Unity. About doing good in the world. But he had been lying.

"Saskia," I said eventually. "Do you think she's heroic? Successful at fighting evil and all?" Could a cold-blooded murderer also be a hero?

I wondered what Saskia's motives had been, exactly. What was it I had seen in her face as I sat across from her, as I looked deep into her eyes? Pain? Regret? Fear? What had she wanted from me? Forgiveness?

Was what she had done evil? All of it? Part of it? I thought so, but I – I had done nothing. What was that? Who was I to judge?

"Is that what you think?" James asked. "That Saskia is a hero?"

"I don't know," I said. I turned back towards the window, and watched the darkness outside the car.

She had participated in Unity, understanding what she did. And then, she had risked her own life, and her future, to shut it down.

She had made love to my brother – my wicked brother – and then murdered him.

There was something I didn't know, and maybe never would, about her relationship with Patrick Leyden.

She had tried to keep me out of Unity. In her weird way, she had tried to protect me. Maybe.

She was friendless. She was alone. She was facing all kinds of court trials – as witness, as defendant. It would go on and on. She'd said she had a lawyer. What kind of a life would she have from now on?

I didn't understand her. I had never understood her. Behind that lovely face, she was layer upon layer of complexity. If I were to try to paint her, I wouldn't know where to begin... I was even more afraid of her now, in truth, than I had been before. She was a dangerous girl, Saskia Sweeney.

No. A dangerous woman. A woman.

Like me.

Compulsively I said, "Will she be all right? What will happen to her, James?" I hadn't meant to say his name. It just came out.

James didn't appear to notice. He said, "It's going to be rough on her. She'll need to be strong. And – she's going to need a friend, Frances. Badly."

I couldn't speak for a moment. Then I said, "You don't know what you're asking."

"Maybe not," said James.

We finally broke free of traffic and the car picked up speed. We sat in silence for the remainder of the drive. But as we entered the outskirts of Lattimore, James said abruptly, "Frances? I want you to know something. You're going to be a very intriguing, very attractive, and very unique woman. Well, you already are. I hope you know that. The man you decide to love someday – when all this is over and you've come into yourself – will be very lucky. That is very clear to me."

He didn't look at me. And he didn't say anything else. I knew for sure then that he did know how I'd felt – how I still felt – about him.

He was trying to make me feel better. In the midst of everything that had happened, he was trying to make me feel better about that one thing. I swallowed hard.

Maybe James already had a lover in his life. Yvette? No, somehow I couldn't imagine that; and, rightly or wrongly, I felt I'd have known when I saw them together. But there was a world of women out there.

And yes, I was one – or nearly one – now, now and not "someday", now and not "when I was older". But that didn't matter. *That* was very clear.

James pulled the car on to the Pettengill campus and stopped in front of my dorm. It was just dinnertime, and there was no one in sight. I was a little late to meet Andy, I thought, but I knew he'd wait. I moved to open my door.

"Frances, just one minute," said James.

I turned back and, astonishingly, he reached over and took my left hand. His hand was warm, dry. It enfolded mine, and I felt my entire body go still. I looked at him warily. I wanted to run. I wanted – *wanted* – things I couldn't ever have—

He lifted my hand to his lips and kissed it once, gently, in the very centre of my palm. Then he folded my fingers round the kiss and let go. "Goodbye," he said. "Be good. And, Frances?"

I was feeling as if I'd been kicked, hard, in the stomach, and it wasn't the cramps. I could barely breathe. "What?" I said. The word was almost inaudible.

"I meant what I said a few minutes ago. I meant every word of it."

I felt my shoulders shift uneasily. I could feel the intensity of his gaze. Even in the dark I knew what it said. *You.* A lie? Or not?

I got out of the car. My whole hand seemed to throb. I had just been kissed, sort of, even if it was farewell. The world was black. It was grey. It was unknowable.

I stood on the steps of the dorm. James was still there, in the car, waiting.

With my other hand, the hand he hadn't touched, I waved once and saw James lift his hand in return. I saw his head move in a nod.

I didn't watch James drive away for ever. I let my feet take me, automatically, to meet Andy for dinner.

35

After dinner I returned to my room. I knew I should go to bed early; Andy and I were catching the 6:30 a.m. bus to Boston. Carefully I put the maps of Boston, the bus and subway schedules, and the "Debbie" notebook that I'd started with Andy into my backpack. I planned to take notes tomorrow on everything we did and everyone we talked to. I would also get a list of all the women's shelters in Boston so that we could call them, one by one.

Andy was hopeful, almost ebullient, about our search plans. Being with him at dinner, watching his face as he talked about Debbie, had made me feel a tiny bit less numb. I took the notebook back out and looked at the picture of Debbie that Andy had taped there. She looked like an ordinary, plump, middle-aged woman, but she'd ducked her head a little and hunched into her shoulders as if she feared the camera might attack her. *We will try,* I told the picture silently. *I will try my very best to find you and help you.*

I put the notebook away again. I set the alarm clock. It wouldn't hurt if I went to bed now. But I didn't know if I could sleep. Behind the barriers I'd set up I could feel my brain shaking, my pulse pounding. If I turned out the light, if I lay still in bed, would I be attacked by all I'd learned today?

It might take you years, James had said.

I was overwhelmingly aware all at once of the mirror in the corner, on the wall, still draped in black. I ought to take it down now, I thought. Its purpose was over. It and its black mourning cover should come down. The Frances who had put them there was gone. Gone for ever – even if I didn't quite know who she – who I – had become.

Was becoming.

Still, I didn't take the mirror and the fabric down. Instead I got undressed and into my pyjamas. I carefully put away the new white cashmere sweater, unable to resist giving it one gentle stroke before closing the drawer on it. I went to the bathroom, Mr Monkey in hand, and briskly flushed away the remains of Daniel's marijuana. As I came out of the toilet stall, I was surprised to run into Tonia Mack, also in pyjamas, brushing her teeth. We smiled shyly at each other and she murmured something about not knowing I was another person who liked to go to bed early sometimes. Then we both scurried back to our rooms. I set the empty Mr Monkey on top of my bookcase.

The mirror looked at me again, and this time I looked straight back at it. I crossed the room and stood before it. Slowly I drew off its black silk covering. Then, without having planned to do so, I went back for my new white sweater. White, the colour of mourning for Buddhists.

I put it over my shoulders. Then I took a deep breath and

murmured aloud the Mourner's Kaddish, the Jewish prayer for the dead. *Yit-gadal V' yit-kadash sh'mey raba...*

I said the entire prayer, astonished at myself because I hadn't realised I knew it by heart. When the last words fell from my lips, I hunched my shoulders beneath the white sweater, put the black silk to my face, and wept.

I cried, not for the little boy I'd loved, but for the adolescent boy I hadn't known at all. The one who had tried to convince me that he knew everything there was to know about serving others, about love, about humanity, about giving. But Daniel had known nothing about any of it. He had been an illusion. My illusion.

You are so naïve, Frances.

I cried until I was empty.

Then I looked into the uncovered mirror, at the face that now seemed a little less unfamiliar. I examined her – my – tear-marked face, runny nose, and swollen eyes. I looked at the cloud of hair. I thought of the woman's body that was mine, that I could feel under my hands...

I remembered the years of wishing that I had a face and body like Saskia's. What did Saskia see, I wondered now, when she looked into a mirror? It was so odd to understand, fully and completely, that it wasn't and never had been what I had thought.

At some point, I knew, there were going to be tears in me for her as well. I could feel them deep within me. Had James known that somehow? Was it why he had said to me that she would need a friend?

James. Gently I closed the fingers of my left hand round the ghost of his kiss. I drew air deeply into my lungs, and let myself hear his words again. Intriguing. Attractive. Unique. I looked again into the mirror. Did I dare believe him?

The mirror was of course too small to use to see myself full-length. I was a little relieved; the thought still frightened me.

I remembered my broken promise to myself, seven years ago in Bubbe's bathroom, to climb up on a stepstool and look at my naked body in the mirror above the sink. Maybe it was, after all, a good thing that I hadn't looked then. Ms Wiles – even if she wasn't really an art teacher, even if she had betrayed me with lies – had told the truth about one thing. If you think you already know what you're looking at, you might not see what's really there.

I had been blind for a long time.

Freak. Dwarf.

Intriguing. Attractive. Unique.

I looked into the mirror and I saw Frances Leventhal. She gravely looked back out at me.

Soon I would fulfil that seven-year-old promise. I would look straight on, fully and truly and completely, at myself. Like an artist, like a grown-up, like a woman. I would see what was really there. Who was really there. Not tonight, but soon. Soon.

And maybe – maybe I would even dare a self-portrait. Maybe that way I could begin to learn who I was, and what I believed.

I was tired, I realised abruptly. So overwhelmingly tired. Too tired to think, too tired to move. I put both the black fabric and the white sweater away in a drawer. I couldn't stay upright another second.

It was such a relief to be in bed in the dark... to be warm beneath the covers... to have plans for tomorrow... to know suddenly that I was going to sleep deeply tonight. And, just as I was drifting off, a voice in the back of my head whispered that if I asked my father to help Andy and me find Debbie, he would. He would try to help if I asked.

I curled my hand round James's kiss. Then, dreamless, I slept.

ACKNOWLEDGMENTS

Most of Daniel's Buddhist quotes are from *The Dhamma-pada*, a popular and frequently translated anthology of 423 verses from the Theravada Pali Canon.

I would like to thank Kathleen Sweeney, Franny Billingsley, Deborah Wiles, Dr John Leventhal, and especially Richard Pettengill for allowing me to purloin parts of their names.

Joanne Stanbridge talked to me about practising art and what the ideal studio should smell like. Victoria Lord and Jennifer Jacobson provided expert help with sticky points of information.

Thanks go to Kimi Weart for sharing some of her memories of growing up with a family background like Frances Leventhal's.

I owe much gratitude to Conrad O'Donnell for his detailed reading of and comments on the first draft, and for helping figure out the details of the thriller plot.

Finally I'd like to thank my editor, Lauri Hornik, for her support, trust, probing questions, advice, and guidance throughout the process of writing this novel.